Alex

George and the Dragon

A grubby tale of the Eighties

Simon Coventry

Hope you think it's as 'timic' as others do !

Simon

ZEBU

Published by Zebu 2014

First published August 2014 for Kindle
2nd Edition for Kindle and print October 2014

All characters, companies, locations and cars are fictional

Cover photo Simon Zebu

ISBN-13: 978-1502466044

For all the dragons out there

Contents

I wanted to kill the Dragon.

"You go and have a good time," she'd said. "Don't concern yourself for a minute that I'm going to have to work all afternoon. You just sod off and enjoy yourself. And mind you don't come back drunk."

Fat chance, I thought. The last time I'd gone home drunk she'd persuaded her dear brother Alf to take some time off from breaking kneecaps to come round and give me a severe talking-to. The chat had stopped short of physical violence but I was left in no doubt at all how the family expected me to treat their darling little Beryl.

"Look," I said to her. "If you're so worried about what I do, why don't you come with me to the wedding?"

"What, on Raymonde's day off? Leave Sandra in charge of the salon? You must be joking," she replied. "I'd lose all my clients in one afternoon. Besides which, if you'd wanted me to come to this wedding, you would have told me about it sooner than this morning."

Now there she had me. I'd got the invite from my nephew Bob about a month before, but because he'd sent it to the warehouse and we were in the middle of the stocktake, what with one thing and another, it had slipped my mind until he'd rung the previous evening. Still I was buggered if was going to admit that, so I said:

"Look Beryl, it's not my fault you never listen to anything I say, is it? I told you about this do last month. You just chose to forget because Bob's my family."

"Just because my family's a bit difficult and you can't handle that, doesn't mean I have anything against yours."

"A bit difficult," I spluttered. "A bit difficult! Your bloody brothers have threatened me with broken limbs so often I feel like I'm already in plaster."

"That's just their way. They're not nearly as bad as you make out. You're pathetic."

"Listen to yourself Beryl, 'not as bad', not as bad! They're way bloody worse. They're a curse and they've not even got the compensation of being funny. I think we'd both be better off without them."

"You think what you like sunshine," she came back at me. "I just know I've got a business to run and you are treading on very thin ice."

And with that she swept out of the room in a cloud of Caleche. I heard the door to her room slam. There wasn't any point in following her, I'd just get more of the same so I got my overcoat and went out to the Jag.

I was angry with myself for needling her. I should have stayed calm. I drove fast towards Harpenden, or should I say I tried to drive fast. The trouble with the Jag is that no matter how angrily you drive it, the bloody thing just wafts along, all bloody composure. I sometimes wish I had a Cortina again.

I got to the wedding a bit early, so I parked down the other end of the High Street from the Register Office to do some homework as I walked past the shops.

I found a carpet shop and stopped to see what they were selling for how much. They had most of the standard Axminsters and broadlooms, shag-piles and sculptureds, their prices weren't bad either. Not as good as mine, but still not bad for a poxy little high street shop with no big buying power. I made a note of the name of the place and made my way to the wedding.

To tell you the truth I didn't notice much of the ceremony. I find people getting married somewhat depressing. I could see that Bob's bird looked all right, but then again Beryl had seemed like a good catch in her time. It doesn't take much for them to change for the worse. In Beryl's case it had taken something a bit more than dirty socks on the floor.

Everything had been bloody wonderful when we'd met at the dances. We were good at dancing and just clicked. Then I got her up the duff and her family stepped in to persuade me to propose and marry within a month. There's not much you can do to defend yourself against a family of bloody gangsters. Still, we were happy together until she lost the baby and was told she'd never have any more. Somehow, the fault for all that was laid at my door.

I switched off and thought of ways I might be able to get rid of Beryl without incurring the wrath of her ever-loving family. Not that I'm after going off with some other bird, you understand. I could just do with some peace and quiet in my life. Somehow you don't get any time to just sit and think with a woman like that around.

People were moving around me and I realised it was time for the pictures and the piss-up. I moved out with the crowd and hovered in that limbo-land of nobody knowing where they should be standing or where they should go until some bright spark separated the immediate relatives from the rest of us and sent us lot down the road to the Brightman's Hotel to wait like wallies with our little boxes of confetti while the main characters got their pictures taken.

After all the official crap, it looked like being a pretty good class of do. There was bucketfuls of champers and a buffet table groaning with plenty of red meat and poached salmon with only a token bowl or two of that bloody awful salad stuff.

I got stuck in, made the right noises to the loving couple, nodded to a few people I knew and settled in for an enjoyable afternoon without the Dragon killing joy left, right and centre.

With a couple of glasses of bubbly inside me, I was surveying the room and listening to the band, when I saw these two birds over by the wall looking at me and giggling. I discreetly checked my flies while pretending to be engrossed by the buffet and looked again. Sure enough they were still at it. I looked towards them and raised an eyebrow. One of them lit a cigarette, said something to the other and came over to me.

"Do you want a dance?" she said. Now this sort of took me by surprise. Fifteen years of the Dragon had blunted my enthusiasm for chasing women, so to have some bird in her twenties asking me to dance threw me a bit off balance. Not that I'm so slow or stupid to turn down an offer like that. You need to be a quick-thinker in my line of business.

"Yeah, love to darling," I said, parking my glass on the table behind me. I led her out onto the floor and we cruised in and out of the other couples. Much to my surprise she could actually dance. When I was younger everyone could, but now they just seem to shuffle at each other.

As we passed her friend she called out:

"There, I told you so!"

"Okay Trish," the friend replied as we twirled out of earshot. "You win."

"What's all that about then?" I asked her. I hate conspiracies. "What have you won?"

The number ended raggedly catching us both off balance. I reached gratefully for my drink. I may have been a good dancer in my youth but I was suddenly out of breath and I could feel drops of sweat on my forehead.

"Out of practice?" she laughed.

"No," I said. "It's just a bit warm in here, isn't it?" I could do without a conversation about how old and unfit I must be.

"What was all that about winning?" I asked again.

"Winning?" She looked puzzled, then she laughed again. "Oh that! That was just a little bet I had with my friend Laura. She said there was nobody in the whole place who could dance more than one proper step without falling on their face. I spotted you."

"But I wasn't dancing."

"No, but I knew from your feet."

"Bollocks," I said. "You just made a lucky guess." But I have to admit I was flattered. Okay, it was just a stupid bet between a couple of bored girls at a wedding. Bored maybe, but now I came to look at her properly I could see this one was a cracker.

Isn't it funny how after a few years of living with one woman you stop noticing all the others. You just get kind of numb.

"Do you fancy another dance?" I said, as casually as I could, feeling the mood rising.

"If you feel up to it," she smiled. "Sure grandad." I nearly unleashed the reflex anger then bit my tongue remembering this wasn't the Dragon.

"I think the old ticker might hold out for another few minutes." I said, forcing a smile.

She laughed again. That laugh was beginning to get to me. It was ages since I'd heard a woman laugh out of pleasure, not malice.

We danced another couple of numbers and to tell the truth I think I probably did have a couple of mild heart attacks but I didn't really notice and certainly didn't give a toss. We'd dance a couple, rest a couple, have a drink, have a smoke, chat a bit, then I'd have a quick dance with Trish's mate Laura. All very civilized you might say, but this innocent fun would have been quite enough to put me in solitary for a month had the Dragon seen it. Had the Dragon seen what was passing through my mind I'd have been chatting to her brothers.

The upshot of all this was that I managed to persuade Trish not only that I would be her best way of getting home, but also that Laura would probably be better off on her own. I don't know what Laura had done to deserve this, but I wasn't about to side with her at this stage of the game. It may have been a long time past but I could still remember the horrors of trying to separate two girls once they're both in the car.

So while Laura went to the ladies, Trish and I sneaked out of the hotel without saying good-bye to the happy couple.

Now I hate to get lyrical at this stage, especially considering what was going through my mind, but we walked arm-in-arm through the warm drizzle towards the car, her head leaning on my shoulder, her left leg in step with my right.

"Now I wonder which is your motor," she said. "I like to try and place a man by his wheels." She muttered the makes as we passed by them, but none seemed to qualify. She certainly knew her cars.

When we got to the Jag she broke loose.

"This must be the one," she said, standing by the passenger door with a grin on her face. I pulled the keys out of my pocket.

"Spot on," I said.

"Really?" she said, looking at me carefully. I unlocked the door for her.

"Mmm," she said as the door swung open and the leather beckoned. "I'm not often wrong you know."

I got in and started the engine.

Now I have to admit that when we drove off down the street I didn't have much idea of how to play this scene, being somewhat out of practice at this sort of thing.

It was chucking it down as we left Harpenden, and I was doing some hard thinking about how I might be able to persuade Trish to stop for another drink at a hotel. See how my luck went from there. Nice brandy in the lounge, check in while she went to the ladies and then casually mention at the appropriate moment that we could go upstairs if she fancied. Get a good room mind, no rubbish. Yeah, that would do the trick. I started to imagine a night of raw passion with room service. I didn't seriously think it was on the cards but there's no harm in dreaming.

I tried to think if I'd passed any hotels on the way to the wedding. I couldn't remember any. Not one. Then I remembered a contract we'd done the previous year for one. Posh place too. The carpet they were replacing was still in good enough nick for most other hotels. In fact I made a bob or two extra on the job by flogging bits and pieces of it to guest houses and the like as 'shop-soiled'. The Monarch Hotel that was its name. It was up this way for sure.

But where the bloody hell was it? Big country house up a proper driveway it was. Big lions on the gateposts with lodge houses on each side of the gate. It wasn't on this road, I would remember passing it on the way. It was round these parts somewhere though.

Just then I got a sharp pain in my groin. I tried to keep

my eyes on the road, watering as they were. I glanced down. She'd grabbed my parts through my trousers and was squeezing hard.

"What the hell are you doing for Christ's sake?" I yelled, wincing with pain. "Let go, let go, let GO!"

"Not till you apologise," she said quietly.

"I'm sorry, I'm sorry!" I shouted. She let go. I felt more relieved than when Beryl's brothers left after a family visit. I swallowed hard.

"Gordon Bennett," I said. "What did I do?"

"You ignored me," she said. "You haven't said a word since we got in the car. I don't like being ignored. I thought you were a lively one. Maybe I was wrong."

"Okay," I replied. "Perhaps I was a bit quiet but there was no call for doing that. It bloody hurt you know. Besides which I may not have been talking to you, but you can be bloody certain I was thinking about you. You, and the Monarch Hotel."

"And the dancing eh?" She asked, all innocent.

"Yeah," I said. "Something like that."

"I'm sorry I hurt you," she said "I'd better make sure I haven't damaged anything." And with that she slipped my flies open, slid her hand in and started feeling around inside.

I was too surprised to say anything. I thought at first she was about to crush me again but then I realised she wasn't. She certainly wasn't doing that. Squeezing maybe, but ever so gently.

"Hmm," she murmured. "There doesn't seem to be any permanent damage, does there?" she asked as she withdrew her hand.

"There will be," I gasped. "If you stop now."

"Oh, forgiven me already have you?" she pouted, leaving her hand on my leg. I caught her drift.

"No." I said, trying to sound convincing. "You'd have to do more than that to get off the hook."

"Oh really?" she said. "Well how about this?" And she put her hand back in my trousers, pulled out the contents, leant over and buried her head in my lap.

Now, to most blokes, driving a new Jag on a rainy night while having a blow-job from a beautiful girl would be their idea of heaven. It wasn't. First off, I was terrified that we'd go over a bump and I'd lose half my wedding tackle. I thanked God that we were in the Jag and not that bloody old Cortina.

Then there was the concentration problem. Every time I started to enjoy what was happening the car started weaving all over the road. I'd think about the driving for a minute and then suddenly realise I'd forgotten all about what she was doing. I had to stop the car but there was nowhere to stop.

Just then there was a sign. Lay-by 400 yards. I speeded up. It seemed like an eternity before the damned thing came into view. I swept into it like Stirling Moss into the pits. Too much like, and they don't have wet gravel in the pits. I slammed on the brakes, Trish jerked herself out of my lap, looked out of the screen and screamed. The car slipped, then went sideways, the headlights lit up the trees. There was a sound like Beryl's brothers both cracking their knuckles at the same time and we went arse-first into the ditch.

Trish stopped screaming. The engine stopped, in disgust I

suppose. She looked at me. I looked at her. We were both sliding backwards up the backs of the seats. She started to giggle, then laugh and, God knows why, I started to do the same.

"I think someone's trying to tell us something," she said as we landed on the back seat. She slowly pulled up her skirt and to tell you the truth I couldn't quite believe it. I'd always wondered who bought that gear, and now I knew. I tell you it looked a lot better than in those catalogues. She reached down to my overcharged part.

"It seems a shame to waste it," she said. And quite honestly I had to agree with her.

I'll spare you the intricacies of sex in the back seat of a crashed Jag pointing up into the sky like an anti-aircraft battery. Suffice it to say, that it's bloody difficult to break rhythm with a set of windscreen wipers.

When we'd made the right noises and disentangled ourselves, I switched off the wipers and lights. I lit a cigarette for each of us.

"Have you ever done that before?" she asked.

"What do you mean?" I asked. "Crashed a car, screwed, or lit two cigarettes at the same time?"

"Screwed."

"Course I have. I'm a married man. Beryl might be an old dragon, but she does have her moments of passion." About once a year, I added silently to myself. "Why? Something wrong?"

"Maybe you're just out of practice," she said. "Let's try again, shall we?" Bloody hell, I thought, it's one of those nymphos the lads at the warehouse are always talking about.

17

"Give us a chance love," I said. "You're not going to get much life out of Percy for a little while yet."

"Ah," she said. "That's just where you're wrong. Come here and do as I say."

And I did, and it worked, and I was getting near the end of the most fabulous screw of my life when there was a knock on the window. I looked up sharply and smacked my head against something hard and sharp. The cigar lighter.

"Oh shit," I said through clenched teeth. "There's someone out there." We looked together. There were two fuzzy shapes just visible through the misted windows. We heard a voice say:

"There's someone in there Jim. Better radio an ambulance."

Police!

"Oh my God," I hissed. We both tried, fairly unsuccessfully, to get our clothes on at the same time. I had just got Trish's skirt caught in my fly zip when the door opened.

"Well, well, well," came a deep booming voice. "Jim," it continued. "Cancel that ambulance and come over here."

"What's up?" came a second voice.

"Get a look at this lot, eh?" booming voice replied. I have to admit I was frozen with terror. Not just the thought of the police either. It had suddenly come to me that this lot was going to take some explaining to the Dragon. Then Trish nearly burst my eardrum.

"Piss off copper!" she yelled. "Show a bit of decency where a lady's modesty's at stake."

"Well, well, well," he repeated. "If it isn't the lovely Trish. Or is it Rita tonight? This your new service apartment then

18

is it?"

"What the hell's he on about?" I whispered.

"Okay," he continued as if he hadn't heard me. "You've got two minutes to get your clothes on." The door slammed. Footsteps crunched on the gravel and I could hear laughing.

"What was all that about?" I asked. "Do you know him, or something?"

"Let's just say he knows me," she replied angrily. "Now just shut up and get your clothes on, eh grandad?"

I was waiting for her as she finished dressing and started looking at herself in one of those little mirrors that women always seem to produce out of thin air, when I twigged.

"You're a tart!" I cried in astonishment.

"Go to the top of the class," she said sarcastically. "Although I'd rather you used the word 'escort'. Now let's go and have a little chat with the nice sergeant before he calls the rest of his mates in on the act, shall we?"

We staggered out of the ditch towards the jam sandwich. Suddenly I was bloody freezing.

"If it makes you feel any better," she said. "What with your car and that, I'll give you that one on the house." I looked back at the Jag. Front end sticking up in the air with the front wheels hanging limply underneath. I was too choked to reply, if there was a reply.

The coppers sniggered as we got in the back of the Rover.

"Now then, Sir," said the sergeant, leaning round towards us, "Would you mind blowing into this device. Always assuming that it was you that was driving the vehicle at the time of the accident." He glanced at Trish. She was busy looking out into the darkness through the rain dribbling down the window.

I blew. He went into the usual legal gobbledegook. I looked towards Trish. Isn't it funny, I thought, how you can go off someone so quickly. Even with the Dragon, it had taken a few months. I wondered whether it was even worth bothering to try and get home.

"...and you'll be summonsed to appear at Harpenden Magistrates Court in the near future. In the meantime we'll take you back to Harpenden and you can make your own way home from there. The station's quite handy for you isn't it Trish?"

It was a bloody nightmare getting a taxi at midnight in Harpenden. All the way back the driver told me about his Open University course, but I wasn't really listening. I was running through explanations in my mind. None of them sounded in the least bit convincing. As the car swung into my road, I decided to tell her what actually happened. It was so unlikely, she probably wouldn't believe me at all. It might make for a grisly couple of days but then maybe she'd throw me out and then I'd be shot of her. Hoo-bloody-ray!

I paid the driver and even wished him luck with his studies. Then, taking a deep breath and counting to three, I went into the house.

It was dead quiet and all the lights were off. I crept through to the lounge to get myself a well-deserved drink. I'd just taken off my shoes when I heard this whirlwind start upstairs.

"George? Is that you George?" Footsteps thundered down the stairs. "George, if that's you, where the hell have you been?" She appeared in the doorway. The sight of that un-corsetted mass, barely hidden by a vast pink satin dressing gown, made me swallow drily. My resolve almost disappeared. Then I thought, George, you've only got one chance. Give it to her straight. I opened my mouth to start but she beat me to it.

"Why the hell couldn't you have rung, eh? I've been worried sick about you. You've been up to no good haven't you?"

She switched the lights on, took one look at me and was off again.

"What's happened to your head? Have you been in a fight? Serves you right if you have." I touched my head and recoiled sharply. It hurt like hell. How on earth had I done that, I thought. Then I remembered the cigar lighter in the back of the car.

"For your information," I replied, "I had an accident. Smashed the car up."

"Silly bloody sod," she said. She sighed, then went on, "I suppose you could do with a drink." She went over to the bar and started pouring. I mean, for God's sake, there I was ready to weather the worst storm this side of Noah's flood, and she suddenly turns all sweetness and light. I swear I'll never understand women.

"Yes I could, as it happens," I replied. I got up to sneak a glance in the mirror and see just how bad my head was. I'd just caught sight of a horrible great blue mark on my forehead when she turned round.

"There you go," she said, handing me a scotch. "You'd better sit down while I get some ice for that head." And she disappeared off to the kitchen leaving me totally bloody bewildered.

I sat there nursing my scotch, trying to figure out how come Harlow's answer to a cruise missile should turn out to be a dud when she came back from the kitchen with an ice pack, pressed it on my forehead and then sat on the arm of my chair. Now that may not seem like much to you, but the closest we'd sat together all year was in the two front seats of the Jag.

"George?" she said, stroking my neck while pretending to support my head.

"Yeah?" I said warily. Her fingers were making the hair on the back of my neck stand on end.

"The warehouse is doing well isn't it?"

"Yeah," I said, just as warily. Where the hell was this leading, I thought.

"I was doing some thinking today."

"And?"

"And I thought wouldn't it be great for the business if I had a bigger salon." Uh oh, I thought. Here comes the bottom line.

"Have you got enough regulars to support a bigger salon though?" I asked.

"Oh yeah," she replied. "Plenty. I've been talking to some of them, and they'd even be okay if the prices went up a bit. There's more than enough of them to pay the rent and Raymonde needs more space to let his creative juices really flow. I'd just need some re-investment to get the new place kitted out."

"How much?"

"Well I haven't quite worked it all out yet, but I shouldn't have thought it'll come to more than ten thousand," she said. So there was my choice: cough up the ten grand or I'd never hear the end of today. Not from her nor any of her bleeding family. I shut my eyes to think.

There was no reason why any of them should ever know about Trish, but that still left the crash and the drunk driving. Now since every other member of her tribe was a getaway driver, that would be pretty hard to take. Of course, there was a third choice. Tell her to stick it, and walk out the door forever. But I opened my eyes and thought why should I give all this up. I've worked bloody hard for this house and all the trimmings. even if it was all in her name. I'd have to spend the rest of my days hiding from her family, start a new business, the lot. I was getting too old to start new businesses in strange towns.

She was right. The warehouse had been doing well lately so I could afford it. It just wasn't worth the aggravation to do anything else.

"All right," I said. "I'll write you a cheque in the morning." I felt all in.

"Oh thanks love," she said. And then she leant over and kissed me. Not a peck on the cheek either. She was ramming her tongue into my mouth so I could hardly breathe. Then she started pawing at the front of my shirt. Oh God. Why did she pick tonight to get all fired up? I tried to prise her off me but she's a big girl, my Beryl. I thought about walking out the door after all, but I was just too damn tired. The only thing I could do was to go along with it, hope it didn't last too long and get to sleep as soon as possible.

That Sunday passed without any major upset. The Dragon was sickeningly sweet all bloody morning. She kept going to the drawer in the kitchen and looking at the cheque inside. Then she'd come and tell me more and more extravagant plans for the new salon. I think I preferred her when she was stamping around the house cutting the air in her path with bitter sarcasm. At least you knew where you were with that.

The previous night had been worse than I'd imagined it would be. She'd finally stopped heaving and groaning after about half an hour, but then she wanted to start talking. Every time I was dropping off, she'd nudge me and want some response to her twittering on about suitable shops and sympathetic streets. I'd finally managed to slip off to my own room when she'd started snoring about three quarters of an hour later.

After lunch she suddenly decided she couldn't wait any longer and had to go and share her news with her mate Stephanie. Stephanie owned a flower shop paid for by her long-suffering husband Carl.

"Why don't you come along with me, eh?" she said. "You and Carl can have a nice chat about warehouses while I talk to Steph about the new salon."

I wondered just how long she'd been thinking about this salon. And another thing, why do women always assume you'll get on with someone just because you're in the same line of business? At one time I'd got on all right with Carl. He played golf to keep out of Stephanie's way and had talked me into trying it once. I bought all the gear and then played so badly Carl and his mates took the piss out of me. I'd loathed him ever since.

"No," I said. "I've got to do something about the car."

"Oh come on George. The car can wait till tomorrow. No one's going to walk off with it. Besides which, how are you going to get there? I'm taking my car."

"Oh shit, yeah," I said.

"And don't think just because yours is off the road you can be borrowing mine all the time."

"Borrowing?" I said. "I bought the bloody car."

"And gave it to me, to do what I liked with, if I remember rightly. And I like to use it," she said, sweeping majestically out of the room. "You'll bloody well hire a car while yours is being mended," she said, sweeping back into the room to collect the cheque from the drawer.

"You want to watch it Beryl," I said. "Or I'll cancel that cheque." She turned on me with contempt.

"You wouldn't dare," she spat as she finally left the room.

I heard the front door slam and the BMW driving away. Ah well, I thought, at least that little set-to had got me out of listening to Carl gloating about his golf club membership all afternoon. I decided to spend the rest of the day being kind to my hangover.

I sorted myself out a large Bloody Mary, turned on the afternoon movie, and settled on the couch with the News of the World. The paper was full of headlines like "Vice Girls Shock" and "Top Businessman Quits After Sexy Revelations". I couldn't find more than three items I could read without sweating.

When the Dragon came back she was all full of herself again. Stephanie must have had a field day filling her head with ideas even sillier than the ones that were there already. Not least of which was obviously a warning to be sweet to me until the cheque cleared. It was bloody un-nerving to have her all over me all evening. I don't think I heard more than half a dozen questions on Mastermind for her wanting to know if I wanted anything.

The only consolation for this was that I could safely say I just wanted some peace and quiet without her flying off the handle about ingratitude and all that. She'd go and sulk on the other couch for five minutes, then start telling me about the new salon, then ask me if I wanted anything again.

In the end I got so fed up I said I was going to have an early night. Unfortunately she got the wrong idea and followed me up to bed. After about half an hour I gave up trying to dissuade her. I realised it would be quicker to get it over and done with.

I had to get another taxi on Monday morning to get to the warehouse. Those blokes are unbelievable. This one was convinced I wanted to know everything about hang-gliding. I mean, perhaps it's interesting to know that a business rival has taken it up, but beyond that, I think the less we hear about it the better, especially on Monday mornings.

I was so wound up at the prospect of having to get another one home that night that I made Maureen spend an hour trying to track down a Jag to rent. When she finally found one, she told me it was going to cost a ton and a half a day to hire it. A ton and a half a day! Sod that, I could buy four of them on the never-never for that.

Maureen spent the next few hours sorting out a tow-truck for my Jag. It was only going to take a week to repair, they said. I decided to use cabs for a week and buy some earplugs.

I was right pissed off with everything by mid afternoon. We had too much stock, sales had been well down over the weekend, and that ten grand winging its way into the Dragon's salon account started bothering me. I got on the blower to try a few contacts of mine, but no one had so much as a sniff of anything big coming up.

Then the phone rang.

"Hello, is that Healey Carpets?"

"Yeah, yeah," I said. "George Healey speaking."

"I have a slight problem with some carpet. I've been told you could do a large contract in a hurry. Is that correct?"

"Certainly is squire," I said. "Who am I talking to?"

"Ah yes. My name is Freeman. I am working on behalf of McCain Sullivan and Partners."

"So what's your problem Mr Freeman?"

"Well, as you may or may not know, McCain Sullivan and Partners are a large American firm of investment trust brokers."

"Yeah, and?"

"They have a big branch here in the City which is due to be officially opened by the Queen next Monday."

"Yeah." I said. "How nice for you. What's your problem?"

"Well, the fact of the matter is that we need the entire building re-carpeted by Sunday."

"So what size are we talking about here, Mr Freeman?"

"Oh," he said casually. "About a hundred thousand square feet."

"You're kidding," was all I managed to say. My legs went weak. That's eleven thousand or so yards, I thought. At ten quid a yard, give or take a bob, I could make three a yard for myself. That's over thirty grand clear profit!

"Of course if you can't cope with this size of job, I quite understand. It is rather a tight schedule after all."

"No, no. I mean yes Mr Freeman." I could do without this one slipping through my fingers. "Of course I can fulfil your requirements," I said. "What's your budget?"

"Well er, within reasonable limits of course, basically, whatever it takes." They were over a barrel.

"And I suppose," I said sarcastically. "That it's all got to be royal blue?"

"Well er, as a matter of fact, yes, the board have decided along those lines." Gotcha. I just happened to know exactly who had a factory-load of Midnight Blue that he'd been trying to off-load for the last six months. They wouldn't know the difference, especially if they were Yanks anyway.

"You do realise, Mr Freeman, that a specific colour is going to up the cost, being as it's a rush job." I covered the mouthpiece while he thought about that one. "Maureen!" I yelled. "Get onto every fitter on our books. Book them all up till Sunday night. Yes, even the dodgy ones. Cowboys, idiots, the lot. Just book them up for Christ's sake."

"Oh yes Mr Healey," he says. "We'll of course make allowances for that, and also the fact that we're in occupation."

"Do what?" I nearly cried.

"Oh yes, I thought you realised. We've been using the building for six months now, that's why we need the new carpet. You'll have to do the fitting outside office hours."

"Can't you just close the place for a week?" I asked.

"Mr Healey," he said, all patient, like he was talking to a kid. "If McCain Sullivan and Partners closed down for a day, millions would be lost. To close for a week would probably precipitate a Sterling crisis. No one, least of all the Queen, would thank us for that."

"Okay, okay," I said. "Hold on to your hat, it was just a thought." I covered the phone again. "Maureen! Make that all night, every night till Monday morning."

"What I suggest, is that you come up to the City, now, and

we can agree a contract immediately. While you're on your way, our legal department can draw up a draft contract and we could have the whole thing tied up this evening. I presume you would like to start as soon as possible?"

"Well yeah," I said. "But I've got to figure out the logistics of the job first."

"Fine," he said. "You bring whoever you need with you now and you can do all that while we sort out the contract. We'll expect you in a couple of hours." He rang off.

I put down the phone. Shit! Panic. I got hold of Eddie and managed to get an option on his factory-load of Midnight Blue, while Maureen tried to find some wheels. Then I tried to find out where Keith, my best fitter, was working. Turned out he was doing some dodgy job as a favour for someone. I got the number out of the yard boy by threatening to fire him, then phoned the number.

"Whatever the fuck you're doing there, leave it right now and come back here," I shouted.

"What shall I tell her?" he bleated. "I'm halfway through fitting."

"Tell her your mum's died, just get over here!"

"It is my mum, Mr Healey," he whimpered.

"Well, tell her I've died then." By this point, I bloody nearly had. Maureen couldn't get a car for love or money, all the taxi companies were engaged and the last train to London for two hours had just left.

When Keith walked into the office, I grabbed him and marched him to the door.

"I sincerely hope the van has got some diesel in it," I said as

31

his nose opened the double doors for us. "You're doing some overtime tonight in London, gratis, to make up for your doing jobs on my time."

The van was a bloody pigsty. No, I tell a lie, it was like a plague. Fag-ends and carpet tacks everywhere and the floor littered with plastic cups, most of which were bleeding trails of congealed coffee. I sat on the passenger seat and felt my suit trousers ripping. Feeling underneath my arse, I found a strip of gripper wedged down the back of the seat. I pulled it out and the trousers ripped a bit more.

"You cunt," I said.

"Oh, terribly sorry about that Mr Healey. We never seem to have the time to clear out the vans properly lately. What with all the fitting we have to do and that. By the way, where are we going?"

"You seem to have enough time to do freelancing on the side, with my materials I might add," I snapped. "Head for London."

So there we were, an hour and a half later, getting close to the city, when I suddenly realised I didn't have an address. That bloody twit Freeman hadn't told me where their bleeding headquarters were. I told Keith to stop at the next phone box. He found two together and pulled up on the pavement right by them.

"Keep an eye out for wardens," I said as I squeezed out through the gap he'd left and went round the front of the boxes. They were both occupied, so I stood there like a wally with the wind chilling my arse through the hole in my trousers. I tried to work out which box I should stand by. One of them had a couple of girls with a copy of the paper and a pile of tens, the other had some bloke rabbiting on in Spanish or Italian or something. I went for the foreigner. Some woman came up and stood near the other box. I scowled at her, then carried on scowling at the foreigner.

After about five minutes, the girls suddenly scooped up their ten pees and burst out of their box jumping up and down, holding a shorthand pad up in the air like it was the F.A. Cup. I made for the door, but the woman was too quick for me. She opened the door sharply against my knee and whipped in like a ferret up a drainpipe. I limped back to the other box, rubbing my knee, and had to outstare some bloke who'd parked himself there.

I managed to get in when the foreigner came out, only to find there were no directories. I rang directory enquiries.

"Directory," the voice said. "What town?"

"London," I said.

"You'll have to ring 142 for London directory," she said, ringing off.

I rang 142.

"Name please," said a voice that sounded exactly the same.

"McCain Harrison and Partners," I said.

"And what address is that please?"

"That's what I want to know."

"There's no listing for that name."

"There must be," I said. "It's a bloody great company in the city."

"Well there's no listing. Have you got the right name?"

"Of course I've got the right bloody name," I shouted. There was silence for a second.

"There's a McCain Sullivan and Partners in EC2," she said. "The number is 846 9562."

"I don't want the bleeding number," I said. "What's the address?"

"78 Cheapside, EC2," she said. "And there's no need to be so rude. We do our best you know."

I slammed the phone down and pushed my way out of the box. I was just in time to see a yellow peril writing out a ticket.

"Oi!" I yelled. "You can't do that, we're delivering."

The warden looked up.

"Not that I can see," she said, deadpan. "Besides which, this area is No Loading as well as No Parking." She put the ticket in its bag and slipped it under the wiper. I took it off, threw it on the ground and got into the van. Keith was nowhere in sight. There was a knock on the window and I wound it down to have some hooray thrust the muddy ticket at me.

"I say," he said. "You appear to have dropped this."

"Well I don't want the bloody thing," I said.

"Want it or not," he said, peering into the cab and turning up his nose. "We'd rather not have our streets looking like that." He flicked the bag into my lap and walked off.

"Stuck-up nosy Parker!" I yelled after him.

Keith sauntered across the road towards me.

"I thought I told you to keep an eye on the van," I said.

"Yeah, I know," he replied, getting in. "But I'd run out of cigs."

"Well that's coming out of your wages sunshine." I said, shoving the ticket under his nose.

He threw me a filthy look.

"At least I take the address with me when I go somewhere," he said.

"I'll have less of your lip," I said through clenched teeth. "Just remember who pays your wages, eh? 78 Cheapside, EC2 and get on with it."

"Where's that?" he said.

"I don't bleeding well know," I said. "Haven't you got a map?" He groped around in the door pocket.

"I don't think Watford and surrounding area comes down this far."

"Haven't you got an A to Z?"

"No."

"Well go and bloody buy one then."

"Where?"

"Oh for fuck's sake Keith, try the shop where you just got your fags."

"Oh, right you are," he said. "Good idea." He opened the door, then turned back. "Have you got any money? I just spent my last on the fags."

I reached into my back pocket and felt the rip in my trousers tear some more.

"Bugger it," I cried. "Now look what you made me do. How the hell am I expected to negotiate this contract with the arse hanging out of my trousers?"

"I dunno Guv," he said, smirking. "No, tell you what, there's some carpet tape in the back there, you could stick them together with that. Hang on a minute, I'll get it for you."

"At last," I said with relief. "A glimmer of common sense fights its way to the surface." I gave him some money and he went to get the map while I clambered into the back of the van. I took off my trousers and was trying to find something to cut the tape with, when there was a knock on the windscreen. I looked up. There was a copper standing there.

"Oh shit," I groaned. I leant over the back of the seat and wound down the window.

"Kindly move the vehicle, Sir," he said. "You're causing an obstruction."

"Er, yeah, well," I said. "The driver is just across the road. He'll be back in a sec." I hoped to God he couldn't see below my waist, and I had to stop him from wanting me to get out. "Perhaps you can help us actually, officer. We're trying to get to Cheapside EC2, do you know how to get there?" I had to keep him talking till Keith got back. It was more than I could bear, the thought of being caught by a copper with my trousers down in the back of a vehicle for the second time in a week.

The copper rabbited on for a couple of minutes, giving me directions, but I wasn't taking any of it in. I kept looking across the road to see if Keith was coming. After a bloody age, he did appear. Not before I'd suffered at least a couple of heart attacks in the meantime.

"Great, thanks a lot officer," I smiled nervously. "Okay let's go Keith." I rolled up the window. "What the hell kept you?" I snarled.

"Oh," said Keith. "I didn't know whether you wanted the plain or the colour one."

"Jesus Christ!" I said. "Well I hope you know how to read the bloody thing, as I'm somewhat busy back here." We finally made it to Cheapside and after we'd pissed about looking for a parking space for about twenty minutes, Keith left the van on a double yellow. He swore blind that there were no wardens after five o'clock.

We got pulled up by the doorman who wouldn't let us in, but after a quick call to our Mr Freeman he grudgingly let us go up to the sixth floor.

The lift was one of those flash jobs with mood lighting and a tinted mirror but we still looked like a couple of tramps despite all that. I ran a comb over my head but it didn't make much difference. I hate places that make you realise how badly dressed you are. It didn't help having that rip in my trousers.

Some toff in a suit and one of those coloured shirts with a white collar met us as the doors opened. He held out his hand, looked at us, then looked at his hand and put it back in his pocket.

"Ah yes," he said. "I'm Freeman. Come this way please Mr Healey."

He led the way down the corridor, looking back nervously now and again as if we were going to walk off with the door handles any minute. We were too busy looking at our feet, working out the quality of the carpet they already had. As far as I could make out, there was nothing wrong with it that a good steam-clean wouldn't put right. Still, that was up to them.

We were led into a boardroom that looked like it had been transported from a stately home. All wood panelling and a ruddy great table big enough to set a swimming pool into. We must have been standing there with our mouths open because a big geezer with cropped hair at the far end of the table got to his feet.

"I see you're admiring the panelling Mr Healey," he said. "We transported it piece by piece from Colesham Hall along with the table." He sounded like Stewart Granger.

"Didn't Colesham Hall miss it?" I asked.

"Didn't have time to miss it," he smiled. "Whole darned place was accidentally demolished two weeks later."

He paused to let this sink in, then went on:

"Hey, enough of the furniture. I'm Franklin B Sullivan and this here is our legal eagle Bob Pevsner."

He gestured to a figure sitting beside him. Mr Pevsner was a nasty looking piece of work with gold glasses and thick, curly black hair. One of those blokes who has to decide where on his neck to stop shaving and start calling it chest hair.

I nodded at Franklin B and his legal beagle.

"Sorry we're late," I said. "This is my chief contract supervisor, Mr Clark." I gestured to Keith and he looked around uncomfortably, obviously unused to the way business is done at such a high-flying level. Not me though. I know how these people work. They like labels. It makes them feel they're getting value for money.

Franklin B looked at Keith, then looked hard at me. His face changed from genial host to Mafia hit-man.

"Okay, let's cut the crap," he said. "You're a small-timer Healey, but we're in a hole. You're the only person we've found who even claims to be able to get us out of it." He laid his hands on the edge of the table and leant towards me.

"We've got a hundred thousand square feet and we'll pay whatever it takes, but if that carpet isn't there when Her Majesty sets foot in this building next week, we'll break your balls Healey. You get me? Now what I suggest is that your chief whatever-he-is goes with Freeman and has a look at the sort of problems you're going to have, while we look over this contract of Bob's."

Freeman led Keith out of the room. Franklin B pointed to the chair next to his and I went round the table and sat there, hoping they couldn't hear the sound of crinkling carpet tape in my trousers.

"What would be the normal price per square yard for this

kind of job?"

I thought about what he'd just said about 'whatever it takes' and plucked a high figure out of my head.

He looked me in the eye and after an uncomfortable pause said: "Now you and I both know that's horseshit. I was going to offer you twice the normal rate to make sure it gets done, but I've just reduced that to 150%. Take it or leave it."

"I'll need twenty percent up front." It almost felt like Dallas, except that I seemed to be on the Cliff Barnes end of things.

"Okay, done. Freeman will sort out a draft but like I said, you screw up…"

Pevsner started going through the contract and it didn't take a genius to see they meant what they said. My balls started hurting at the thought of what they would do if I screwed this one up. As he went on, my balls hurt even more. I realised it was for real, they really did hurt something chronic.

When Pevsner finished explaining the terms, Franklin B turned to me.

"There you go Healey," he said. "A real humdinger huh? You got any questions?"

"Yeah," I said. "Where's the toilet?"

Franklin B burst out laughing.

"Hey," he said. "Surely it's not so bad as that." Then he looked at me again. He stopped laughing and jerked his thumb towards the door.

"Out there bud. Executive John is the second door on the right."

I tried not to run out of the room, but as soon as the door closed behind me I moved like a whippet into one of the cubicles. My underpants had got stuck to the carpet tape on my trousers, but once I'd got that sorted out I pulled the whole lot down to my ankles and stared at my balls.

They were enormous. I mean, usually you just don't think about what size they are, they're just there. Now they suddenly seemed to be the size of a couple of grapefruit. I touched one gently and the pain made me pull my hand back sharply. I sat down on the toilet seat and wondered what the hell I'd done to deserve this.

Somehow I had to get back in to Franklin B and his pet Pevsner and sign that contract. I didn't know what the hell was wrong with me but it wasn't going to get any better sitting in the Executive Toilet of an investment brokers.

I had made up my mind to bear the pain, finish the meeting and get out as fast as possible, then thought I may as well have a slash while I had my trousers down.

I knew something was wrong as I felt the piss coming, but it was too late to stop. I practically screamed as it burst out and I had to look and check that it wasn't razor blades coming out. The pain was horrible. I mean, forget the balls-ache, this was real pain. And it went on and on.

I seem to remember I promised God some pretty silly things in the minute of that piss, but it really was that bad. I sat back when it finished and took some deep breaths then got my balls and the carpet tape back into my trousers.

By the time I got back into the boardroom Keith and Freeman were back, and they all gave me some pretty funny looks. I ignored them, reached for the contract, glanced at the last page and signed on the dotted line with as much dignity as I could summon up.

Keith was being a right pain in the arse as we drove back home.

"Do you know, they've got computer terminals on every single desk in the whole building?" He enthused.

"No Keith, I didn't, and now I do know, I don't give a toss." I said. "Now why don't you tell me something useful like what are the problems on the floor?"

"Well guvnor," he said. "That's the problem."

"What's the problem Keith? For Christ's sake talk sense will you."

"The computers, they're the problem. Every sodding desk in the entire place has a power socket underneath for the computer to plug into. Not only that, but they also have about half a dozen phone sockets each, not to mention some I've never seen before. You can move the desks to lay the carpet but you have to cut and finish round every socket. That's going to add about fifty percent to the time."

I got the impression that Keith was enjoying this little bit of bad news at my expense. I thought for a minute and didn't come up with any brilliant solutions so I said:

"What did the last lot do?"

"What last lot?" he replied.

"How is the carpet that's in there finished," I said. "And why can't someone with your obvious intelligence understand English?"

"That's the thing, you see. All the areas where any real work is done have carpet tiles, it's dead easy to fit them around the sockets."

"Keith, I've been in this trade for twenty years." I hissed at him. "I don't need lectures on the advantages of carpet tiles, all right?"

Shit and corruption, I'd been stitched up. No wonder the bastards couldn't find anyone else to lay their sodding carpet.

"I suppose that's why they suddenly want to get rid of a hundred thousand square feet of carpet. Tiles not good enough for her bleeding majesty."

"That's what Freeman said, yeah. Though not quite in those words."

"I tell you what Keith, if we get through this one there'll be a decent bonus for you."

By the time I got home I was almost feeling sorry for myself. Thank God the Dragon had gone out. There was a note on the table in the lounge telling me she'd be back about eleven. I went upstairs and found another suit, one with baggy trousers. I wondered what to do with the ripped one and decided to chuck it in the bin. There was a bit of room in the dustbin outside, so I crammed it in and went to the lounge for a well-earned drink.

I poured myself a drink and sat down carefully, raised the drink to my mouth and then stopped. The pain in my groin had got a bit better but I wasn't going to chance it, I didn't want to need another piss. Something was going to have to be done about this pain. I decided to call the doctor.

He was out. If I called in the morning the Dragon's ears would be flapping and she'd want to know what was up. I didn't feel like telling her about the intimate details of my pain so I resigned myself to a trip down to the hospital. That meant another taxi, so I didn't get there till about half past nine.

I was paying off the driver and trying to stop him talking about kinetic energy fields when some bloody jobsworth tapped me on the shoulder.

"You can't park there, that's emergency access that is."

"I'm not bloody parking, am I?" I said. "It's not my car, I'm not the driver, and the sooner you chase this maniac away from here the better I'll be pleased."

"Now there's no need to take that tone with me Sir," he replied stroppily. "We have to keep these accesses clear at all times. You wouldn't thank me if the ambulance that brought you in couldn't get near the doors."

"I don't think there are any circumstances where I would thank you for anything," I said as I headed for the entrance.

"I'll remember you!" He shouted after me as I went through the doors. "Bloody anarchist!"

There were two old girls on the desk.

"Can I help?" said one.

"Yeah," I said, "Can I see a doctor?"

"May I ask what for?" she said.

"I've got this pain."

"And where is this pain, Sir?"

"Well, I'd rather not say, it's sort of intimate."

At this the other old girl suddenly got interested in what

was going on. "If you can't say then we can't help you," she chipped in.

"We have to know what department to send you to," piped up the first.

"Oh Jesus, look I've got a pain in my bollocks and I'd like to see a doctor."

"There's no need for that kind of language, thank you Sir," she said huffily.

The second one then said "It's really quite lucky that you came this evening Sir, special clinic is on Mondays."

"What special clinic?" I asked.

"Venereal clinic."

"I haven't got VD," I said. "I'm a married man, it's probably some kidney disease or something."

She turned on a sickly smile. "I think that's for the doctors to decide, don't you? Follow the green line down there and wait with the others please."

I'd never been to a VD clinic before. I found the waiting area and sat down. There were only three other people there. One was a woman who looked like a housewife, the others were spotty oiks. They were all trying to look at me without me noticing.

It took forever for my turn to come. All the time the others were deeply engrossed in five-year-old Reader's Digests or looking at the walls.

I picked up a yellowing Readers Digest and tried to find something funny in the Humour in Uniform page. No luck, so I found an interesting piece of wall that no one else was looking at and tried to count how many coats of paint there were applied one after the other.

Eventually my turn came and I went into the consulting room. The doctor looked at me and started his interrogation. What was wrong, where did it hurt. how long, give a sample. Give a sample! You must be kidding, I thought. I'm not going through that voluntarily. So we seem to be having a little difficulty with the sample, do we Sir? I don't know about you doctor, but for me, yes, it is some difficulty. Never mind we'll do a blood test instead. Oh shit, I hate that. Oh well. Here goes.

"We'll let you know the results of the tests in a day or two's time, but I can tell you now that what you've picked up is gonorrhea. A course of penicillin will soon set you right. Here's a prescription, start taking them immediately, no sex for two weeks, no alcohol, oh, and here's some cards to give to your sexual partners of the last couple of weeks, please give them one each."

Sexual partners, that was a laugh. Oh no. The Dragon. I'd forgotten all about her little thank-you presents for the new salon cheque. Well I wasn't about to give the Dragon a card telling her to go for a VD check-up, and as for Rita or Trish or whatever her name was, she could stuff herself. She probably knew she had it when she gave it to me.

After I got home, I had to make various non-committal evasions to the Dragon. I claimed that I had just got back from London, which led to her discovering that there was a big new contract just started and that in turn led to her knowing all about the Queen opening the building. The rest of the evening was spent trying not to promise her that she would have a ringside seat within touching distance of HRH.

"I expect to get to speak to Her Majesty," were her final words on the subject. "And don't you expect any more of what you had last night, I'm feeling a bit odd."

Well thank Christ for small mercies, I thought.

In the morning the Dragon got up early and spent about an hour in her bathroom. Then she harangued some poor sod on the phone before going out saying she was off to the doctor. I asked what was up but she just gave me the withering look that she saves for girls' problems. I eventually got to work, courtesy of Higgs Taxis whose driver wanted to tell me about the stretch limos he was going to import from the States.

I told Maureen not to let anything except the McCain Sullivan contract get in my way and got straight on the phone. I think I worked harder that morning than I have ever worked in my life. Checking access details with Freeman, talking, cajoling and threatening the freelance fitters I had lined up, getting them to agree to penalty clauses balanced by bonuses, getting the carpet itself delivered, and trying to get some idea of how to deal with the problem of the sockets.

At dinner time I reached for the intercom to get Maureen to make coffee, but then remembered the pain of pissing and took the tablets instead. I was sitting at my desk, trying to swallow the disgusting things without water when all of a sudden I realised what was wrong with the Dragon that made her go to the doctor, and it was not good news for me.

I carried on trying to work through the afternoon, but my mind kept slipping into neutral, and then with a nasty crash

49

of gears onto the problem of the Dragon's appointment with the doctor. If I had passed a dose onto her, life was not going to be easy for me. To tell the truth, it was going to be nigh on to unbearable.

I ran through the options. I could kill myself there and then, but I didn't fancy that when I was just about to make some real money. I could tell her exactly what happened at the wedding and hope that she would see it as a sign that she should perhaps be more caring and less of a cow, but then again I may as well kill myself and deny her the satisfaction of doing it for me. The only other choice, and I may say the only one that would perhaps leave me intact, was to brass it out. Deny everything and make out that she was responsible.

Having made the decision, I felt better, but I can't say I was looking forward to going through with it. I sorted out a few more details of the job, and checked up on the progress of the Jag. It was still going to take about a week. The insurance assessor had seen it and approved the repair.

Being without the car was like a prison sentence. I couldn't cope with any more taxis, hiring a decent car cost a king's ransom, and even when I got the Jag back it wouldn't be the same. They never are once they've been pranged. A thought occurred to me that I might as well replace the Jag now, but maybe not with another Jag. I had always nursed the ambition to have a Roller. The Dragon had nagged me for ages about how we ought to have a Rolls, and I think that was all that stopped me from getting one. Pleasing her was something that was best kept for emergencies, like the cheque on that Saturday night.

That may have been an emergency but what I had now was a bloody crisis. The cost of the thing didn't trouble me too much, with this contract paying me a cool ninety-five grand clear, I could afford a few grand for a decent set of wheels. The money would be rolling in soon enough, and I could put it on my gold card for the moment. I got Maureen to deal with the rest of the day's business and slipped out to get a bus to Gilby and Mather.

No wonder the country's in the state it's in. It took three-quarters of a frigging hour to go 2 miles by bus. The driver was bloody rude just because I had no change and took his anger out on the brakes. It was kind of ironical that I should be going to buy the smoothest car on the road. I promised myself I would never use public transport as long as I lived.

I went towards the glow of the showroom and stood outside, basking in the glow of quality that spilled out of the marbled showroom onto the pavement. After a couple of minutes I noticed that the two smart gents at the desks inside were saying something to each other and giving me sideways glances. I buffed my shoes on my trousers, squared my shoulders and headed for the door.

It was quiet inside, like a church. My steps sounded loud, even on the strip of Wilton that ran between a burgundy Corniche and a British Racing Green Mulsanne Turbo. The carpet led to one of the desks.

"May I help you Sir?"

"Yeah. I want to buy a Roller."

"Ah yes Sir. Well you've come to the right place then. Did

you have any particular Rolls Royce in mind?"

"I want a blue one, Dark Blue mind. And it's got to have a cocktail cabinet. I don't mind what colour the inside is as long as it isn't black." A black interior on a Roller makes it look like vinyl.

"Well Sir, you may have whatever colours and accessories you like. We just need to fill out an order form specifying your exact requirements and the factory will complete the order in due course."

"No, no you don't understand, I want one now. Here. This afternoon." He looked at me as if he was measuring me for a coffin.

"Ah yes, I see. You are looking for a pre-owned example, Sir." The Sir was a touch slower that time.

"Pre-owned, second-hand, call it what you like, it comes to the same thing doesn't it?"

"Yes of course Sir," he said. "If you would care to come out to our pre-owned showroom with me, you will see that these cars are in as-new condition. And, by chance, we do have a royal blue example."

So I went with him to the Rolls Royce equivalent of the back shed. Spotless it was. The floor was cleaner than my warehouse and full of expensive, shiny metal. I followed him between the lines of gleaming cars and then I saw it, my Roller.

Among all the other gleaming machines, mine stood out head and shoulders. Regal, that's how it looked. I just stood there for a while drinking in the sight of it. It had important written all over it. The paint was perfectly smooth, the chrome perfectly mirrored, the glass perfectly clear. I almost ran to it but stopped myself in time and casually sauntered towards it, looking as if I was inspecting it carefully.

It was immaculate, tan inside like all Rollers should be. There was no cocktail cabinet, but there you go, you can't have everything. I sat inside, breathing in the Connolly perfume. I checked out the carpet, and even that was immaculate.

I steeled myself to deal with the salesman. No matter how wonderful I thought the car was and no matter how undignified it might seem to even think about haggling over this motorised perfection, that's what I had to do. I'd never paid full price for anything and I wasn't going to start being ripped off just because the salesman spoke posh and wore a good suit.

As I wafted away from the showroom, I couldn't believe how easy it had all been. To give the bloke credit he barely flinched when I said to put it on my Gold Card. Everything just slotted into place. The insurance broker was in when I phoned and the car had some tax on it anyway, so there I was. In heaven. The pills seemed to have taken the edge off the pain in my trousers, the fitters were all doing their bit and McCain Sullivan's draft was almost winging its way into my bank account.

Just the feeling you need when you've just spent twenty grand on a used car, especially as they wanted twenty-two for it. Still no-one would ever know it wasn't new, it had one of those old number plates on from when they didn't have year letters. Not as good as FU 2 or MR B1G but 5 TER had a certain ring to it.

The traffic didn't exactly melt away in my path, one or two cars waved me out into the queues but the rest seemed to be getting a big thrill out of cutting me up. I suppose they were jealous but I didn't care a damn, I was looking down on all of them.

I was almost looking forward to seeing the Dragon when I got home, or at least looking forward to seeing her face when she saw the car. I pulled into the drive, luxuriating in the sound of the big tyres on the gravel. I was puzzled when I saw not the Dragon's BMW but a Jag I didn't recognise. There was nobody in it which threw me slightly. I wondered why anyone would park their car in my drive.

I got out, locked the Rolls, and walked to the front door. There was something odd about the atmosphere as I went into the house, something not quite right. It felt like someone was there and I immediately thought of burglars. I slammed the door behind me so if there was anybody they would leg it out as soon as possible. I stood still and listened to the silence. If there was someone they were being bloody quiet.

After about a minute of listening I decided that maybe I was wrong so I went into the lounge. As I walked through the door the swivel armchair on the far side of the room began to turn. My heart nearly bloody stopped when I saw it was Alf.

The only thing I could think of was that Alf didn't drive a Jag.

"Hello Alf," I said. "Got yourself a decent car at last then? I wish you'd phone before you drop in." And give me a chance to be out, I thought to myself.

Alf looked at me with cold loathing.

"You've been a naughty boy, haven't you George?" he said.

Now that, in his eyes, could mean anything from not treating Beryl with respect through stealing the crown jewels to shopping one of his brothers to the law.

"I don't know what you're on about Alf. Either get to the point or piss off."

His eyes widened and a look of outrage crossed his face. He got to his feet and walked over to me. He grabbed hold of my coat lapels and put his red blotchy face close to mine.

"You horrible little weasel," he breathed into my face. "You've been dipping your wick where it shouldn't be dipped."

Uh-oh. This was serious. Total denial was the only way out.

"I don't know where you get your information from Alf, but you've got it wrong this time. I don't know what you're talking about. Do you seriously think I'd upset Beryl like that? She's hard enough to live with as it is."

He hit me in stomach and I went faint for a second, then

came to just in time to be sick as I doubled up on the floor. I lay there looking at the pool of vomit as it found its level among the contours of the carpet. It struck me as a pretty good idea to stay there until he had gone, but it seemed he hadn't finished. He grabbed my lapels again and pulled me up.

"You really are a slimy toe-rag," he said, breathing heavily. Despite the awful pain in my gut, I smiled.

"What's up Alf?" I croaked, "Are you getting a bit old for this kind of thing? You used to be able to beat up half a dozen blokes before breakfast." I realised as I spoke that it was not the cleverest comment to make to a professional thug, even if he was getting on a bit. I suppose I was lucky it wasn't his truly psychotic brother Arthur. I lashed out with my knee, hoping to connect with his balls, but he avoided the blow.

He looked even madder then, and closed in to his intimate speaking position.

"You're a cunt, George," he said. "You can't go giving our Beryl doses and expect to get away with it. Now let me save you the bother of denying it because I overheard Beryl talking to Mum."

"She's lying Alf, I swear it. If she had a dose off me I'd certainly know about it, wouldn't I?"

"And I think you probably do," he said with an evil grin on his ugly face as he kneed me in the balls. I screamed and thought I was dead.

When I opened my eyes I saw vomit and smelt vomit. I vomited again and then I listened. There were footsteps upstairs, moving around my bedroom. I ached all over. Where

Alf had kicked me hurt worst, but my ribs seemed to have had his attention too. It hurt to breathe even, let alone move. The footsteps came down the stairs so I just closed my eyes and played dead.

The footsteps went to the front door , there was a heavy thump and then the door opened. It didn't close and it crossed my mind that Alf was a rude bastard. I waited for the noise of the Jag being started but it didn't come. Instead there were footsteps on gravel and then a thump like a car door slamming. There was another thump, and then another.

I opened my eyes and tried to work out what the hell he was doing. I moved very slowly into a sitting position and tried to see out of the window. The sill was too high so I crawled across towards it, every muscle telling me what a bad idea this was. My ribs were on fire, my wedding tackle felt like it would never work again and my head was exploding with every movement.

I finally made it to the window and looked out through the nets. The big dark blur of Alf's body on the far side of the Roller, doing a strange sort of dance. He took a couple of steps, twisted his body, twisted again and there was the thump. The bastard! He was hurting my beautiful new motor.

I forced myself to my feet and staggered out to the front door, shouting as loud as the pain would let me. I lurched through the front doorway and my legs hit something heavy. I fell in a heap on the gravel and saw that I had tripped over my suitcase.

"What the fuck are you doing to my car you bastard!" I yelled at him. He looked over the bonnet at me as he brought down his fist into the middle of it, creating a dent that distorted the reflection of his face.

"Oh what a shame George," he said with the nearest thing to a grin I'd ever seen him wear. "I was hoping this was someone else's and you'd have a lot of explaining to do."

"You stupid, ignorant bastard" I said, feeling tears in my eyes as I struggled to my feet. "You've got no respect for anything, have you?"

"Now watch your lip George, or I'll have to slap you around a little more," he replied. "I've got more respect for most things than you've got for Beryl."

He walked around the front of the car and I thought he was coming to hit me again. I flinched, but as he approached he held out his hand.

"Give me the keys George," he said.

"You're not taking the car," I said. "Are you?"

"The keys, George."

"What do you want them for?" He grabbed me by the shirt and slapped my pockets, then shoved his big hand into my coat pocket, pulled out the keys and pushed me onto the ground again.

He picked up the suitcase, walked to the car, unlocked the boot, put the case in and came back to me. He held up the keys and sorted through them. He frowned and took the car keys off the house key ring, then he closed the front door and locked it.

"Don't worry George, I'm not taking your precious motor, I'm just evicting you," he said as he pocketed the house keys and threw the car keys on the gravel.

"What do you mean?" I said. "This is my bloody house!"

"Was, George, was," he smirked. "If you remember, you signed the house over to Beryl so that you wouldn't lose it if you went bankrupt. Your socks are in the case, now just piss off and keep away from here." He got in his car and leant out of the open window. "Funny old game innit?" he said as he reversed out of the drive.

I gave him a v sign as he drove away and then sat on the front doorstep trying to work out what I felt. My ribs ached with every breath and I felt sick, my head throbbed as if I'd drunk a bottle of whisky in one sitting and my crotch was like a pair of tennis balls, after a match. I got up very slowly and moved like a cripple round to the other side of the car.

Alf had put a big dent in every panel from tail to head light. The bent metal reflected the trees like they were stunted and misshapen. What a petty-minded cunt Alf was, I thought to myself as I opened the doors in turn and looked at all the distorted reflections. The front passenger side wouldn't open. I went back to the driver's side and eased myself gently behind the wheel.

The inside looked the same, felt the same, even smelt the same. The view out was the same, but I knew it wasn't the same. Anyone that saw the nearside would know it wasn't the same. I lit a cig and damn near buckled up with the pain of drawing on it. The pain eased and I wondered what to do.

I looked at the house and wondered why I had been there so long. It was a big comfortable house all right, but it had never been mine. The Dragon had never threatened me with the fact that it was hers on paper. Perhaps she'd been worried that I might have left. Now that would have landed her in it. Nobody to pay for the six-monthly re-decoration, nobody to pay the gas bill, nobody to re-finance her bloody salon. Christ, I almost felt sorry for her.

What was I thinking about? I'd wanted to be shot of her for bloody years. Now her dear family had saved me the aggro of doing it myself. At long last I could lead a quiet life without wondering all the time what her next eruption was going to be about. I was free, and about to be seriously rich.

The first thing to do was to get my ribs looked at. There wasn't much point in being free and rich if I couldn't breathe well enough to smoke. I started the Roller and drove towards the hospital.

It's a good job Rollers have powered everything. Even turning the feather-light wheel sent shafts of pain up and down my chest. I finally eased her into the hospital forecourt and looked for somewhere to park. The notices said "Consultants' Parking Only - Visitors' car park 1/2 mile on left under bridge." Stuff that. I came to a halt in a space marked "Professor Lacock", got out and locked the car.

As I staggered towards the entrance the jobsworth approached me.

"Are you all right Sir?" he asked with concern as he put his arm around but not touching my shoulders, and walked at my side.

"If I was, I wouldn't be here, you bloody idiot," I hissed through clenched teeth.

"Yes of course Sir," he almost saluted, "I just wondered if you needed some help?"

"No, I can make it to the door on my own thank you. Keep your eye on the car though."

"Yes Sir. Of course. It's terrible the vandals that are about nowadays. You can't leave anything anywhere. Just last week there was a robbery from one of the ambulances while they were assisting a patient. Terrible it is, shocking."

"Just do it, eh?"

He smiled and wrung his hands together, started walking

backwards in front of me, and finally stepped sideways out of my path with a last sickening smile like a funeral director at an interment.

I staggered through the swing doors and up to the desk with the two old girls at it. They looked at me coolly as I rested my hands on the front of the desk.

"There's no special clinic tonight," said one of them. "That's only held on Mondays."

"I don't want the sodding special clinic," I said. "I've been mugged and I can hardly breathe."

"There's no need for that kind of language, thank you Mr Healey," she said in her huffy voice.

"Look, if we're on such friendly terms Mrs Elsey," I said looking at her name badge. "Do you think you could do an old friend a favour and get a doctor to have a look at me."

"Sit over there and as soon as a doctor is available you'll be called Mr Healey."

I looked at the chairs and the human debris occupying them.

"Are all that lot going to be seen first?"

"That depends on how serious your injuries are. A doctor will assess the damage and decide how quickly you need attention."

"Well I hope they're as quick as my bloody brothers-in-law," I muttered as I turned to find a seat.

I found a Reader's Digest that looked as if it was a hand-me-down from the VD clinic and sat down between the two least dangerous looking characters there. There was still nothing funny in Reader's Digest and I was looking for something interesting to look at when Mrs Elsey's voice rang out.

"Mr Healey, would you come back to the desk!"

I limped back to the desk.

"What is it then, found a spare doctor?"

"I just wanted to check with you that the details you gave yesterday concerning your address and so on are the same."

"Well, as it happens, they're not."

"Yes, we often find people are embarrassed when they come to the special clinic. Do be good enough to give us the correct details now, on this card please."

"Now look here," I said, getting my rag up. "Those details I gave yesterday were correct, so you can take your sarcastic comments and stick them in your ear."

"So you do live at 63 Blenheim Crescent or not?" she said reading the card.

"I did yesterday but I don't today."

"Oh I see, you've moved," she said handing me a fresh card. "Well just fill out your new address on this new card."

I took the card, got my pen out and stopped to think. Where did I live? Where was I going to sleep? I'd not really thought about that side of the afternoon's events. I thought I'd better put down the warehouse address, but then it would have looked a bit funny, being as it was on a trading estate. I suppose technically I should have put no fixed abode, but I wasn't going to be classed with all the riff-raff that shared that address.

Mrs bloody Elsey was giving me a fishy look so I searched my mind for anywhere that had a bed and sounded possible. Then I got it. A man of my standing, or stooping as it was right then, would be somewhere like The Monarch Hotel. So that's what I wrote.

The address lines were still empty as I handed the card back. She glanced at it and her look turned even fishier.

"That's where you live is it Mr Healey?" she asked, giving me a long-suffering look.

"Yes it bloody well is, at the moment."

She gave me yet another sour look and said

"Such a nice establishment. My niece had her wedding reception there just last month. It must be nice to be able to afford to live there."

"Yeah, well that's what I'm doing."

"I'll fill out the address for you shall I?"

"Yeah, ta." She put the card down on the desk in front of her and started to write. I leant forward to see what the address was and had taken in that it was in Hamble St Peter when she looked up.

"All right Mr Healey, you can sit down and wait now. We'll try to get someone to see you as soon as possible."

I went back to the search for something interesting to look at. I had just given up all hope of there being anything to do while I waited when I realised that if I was going to staying at The Monarch I had better book myself in there. I went to the pay phone in the corner and spent five frustrating minutes with directory enquiries before getting through to the hotel.

I booked a room, put it on the Gold Card and found out how to get there. As I rang off a nurse called my name.

"Mr Healey? Would you come with me?"

I followed her to a cubicle with curtains that she drew behind me.

"Sit down there Mr Healey," she said, pointing to a high bed. "Someone will be along in a minute." She parted the curtains and went out.

After about five minutes a doctor put her head through the curtains.

"Are you the anal fistula?" she asked, then, getting a totally bemused look from me, disappeared.

Another few minutes passed and I have to admit I started to doze off. Lying down eased the pain everywhere. Then just as I was really comfortable another doctor, a bloke this time, came in.

"Hello Mr er..." he looked at the nurse with him.

"Healey," she said. "Chest injuries. He was mugged."

"Mr Healey," he said. "Right let's have a look at you. Take off your jacket and shirt."

I started to struggle with the sleeves of my jacket but the pains started shooting all over my chest. He looked at me and turned to the nurse.

"Help him off with those things will you?" he said. "I'll come back in a minute."

"Hang on a sec doc," I said. "They didn't just kick my chest, they had a go at my parts too."

"What parts?"

"You know, my private parts, my wedding tackle."

"They'd better have," he sighed as he cast his eyes to the ceiling and said to the nurse:

"I can get Harry to do that if you like."

"No, it's all right," she said.

"Well get him stripped and into a gown then."

He left and the nurse started to get my clothes off. Every move she made hurt like crazy, especially when I had to move my shoulders. I gritted my teeth and sucked in and she looked up from where she was pulling my underpants off.

"Sorry Mr Healey," she said brightly.

Finally I was sitting in a gown, with my clothes in a pile on the chair, on my own again. Waiting. Again.

The doctor returned.

"All right Mr Healey, let's have a look at you." He poked and prodded, pushed and pulled until I was nearly screaming.

"Hm," he muttered. "Seems to be a fractured rib or two. There doesn't seem to be anything wrong with your testicles that time won't cure. Better get you up to x-ray for those ribs though. Follow the red line out of here to the right and when you get to the x-ray department give them this." He handed me a piece of paper with a lot of scrawl on it and I staggered off to follow the red line.

After another eternity spent waiting at x-ray, being x-rayed and then waiting again in the cubicle with my clothes the doctor came back. He was looking at some x-rays.

"Here we are Mr Healey just as I thought," he pointed at some grey splodges. "You see there, two fractures. Nurse will strap you up and you can go. Try to avoid anything physical for a couple of weeks and you should be better. If you're not, go and see your GP."

"Is that it?" I was shocked. "Is that the best you can do? No wonder everyone's moaning about the Health Service and going private."

"You're welcome to go private Mr Healey," he said with a stroppy tone. "But the only difference you'll find is that it'll cost more. This is the standard treatment for fractured ribs whether private or on the NHS."

I was beginning to lose my rag at this point.

"Well that may be so doctor," I said. "But it's not the cooking I'm complaining about, it's the service."

He puffed himself up, "That, is all you are paying for when you go private. Now from what Mrs Elsey tells me, you're living at the Monarch Hotel. You'll get all the service you seem to need there, and with any luck it will cost you even more than private medical treatment. I'm a busy man Mr Healey so if you'll excuse me I have sick people to treat. Good day."

He pulled the curtains apart and strode off down the corridor without another word. The nurse looked at me like I was something slimy and bandaged me up with the gentle loving care of a lorry driver with a load of plywood. As soon as she'd finished, she gathered her tackle together and marched out, then immediately opened the curtains again.

"Get your clothes on Mr Healey, you can go home now," she said coldly and disappeared.

Getting my clothes back on was less painful than when they came off, but doing it on my own was bloody near impossible. I finally got my suit on but couldn't get anywhere near tying my shoelaces. I only got the shoes on by cramming my feet into them while standing.

I eventually got my shirt and jacket on, and shuffled off towards the main doors. I was going down the main stairs outside, when I tripped on the bloody laces and fell down the last couple. I was sitting swearing at everything when some bloody ambulance bloke came over.

"Are you all right mate?" he asked, helping me to my feet. "I'll give you a hand inside, get them to take a look at you. You'll soon be feeling right as rain."

"Fuck off," I said as I broke his grip. "You wouldn't get me back in there if I was dying,"

He looked at me stunned for a moment. I turned and started walking towards the car.

"Charming," he shouted after me as I walked away. "People like you don't deserve help."

I felt the wind on my arse as I walked and tried to turn to see what was up. I couldn't turn far enough so I felt with my hand and found a bloody great rip in my trousers. Bloody marvellous, I thought, Alf had better have put a suit in that case. I shambled on towards the car and the helpful shouter continued.

"Serves you fucking well right you rude bastard!"

I got to the car and eased myself gratefully in. I took a couple of breaths as deep as the corset of bandages would let me and started the car. There was a knocking at the window, I looked up and Jobsworth was standing there. The last thing I felt like was a chat with him. I let the window down.

"Well, what do you want?" I asked, blood practically boiling out.

"I was watching the car all the time," he cringed. "I didn't see anyone go near it. It must have been those kids from the estate."

"What the hell are you on about you bloody idiot," I shouted at him.

"Those kids, they must have come over the wall there and done it."

I closed my eyes and took a deep breath.

"Done what for fuck's sake?" I asked. I was getting too tired to shout.

"They've ruined the other side of the car," he said. "Malicious little hooligans. I'd have them all in the glass house, I would. National Service would sort them out. It sorted us out, didn't it?"

I looked at him wearily, "For your information corporal, that was done by a malicious, big hooligan and National Service taught him how to do it."

His face dropped and I closed the window before he could say anything else. I selected Drive and left him standing with his mouth open.

I eventually found The Monarch but it was a right bloody run around. I remembered where Hamble St Peter was but of course the hotel wasn't there. It was up some sodding obscure lane with barely a sign. I eased the Roller along the drive and pulled up in front of the doors, making sure that I had the good side of the car facing them.

Inside, it was one of those hushed-voices reception areas with a blonde girl in a uniform manning the desk: "Can I help you Sir?" she said with a hospitality smile.

I thought she was being sarky then realised not everyone is, all the time, so gave my name.

"Oh yes Mr Healey, you phoned. Do you have any bags?"

"I've got a case in the car." I was about to explain how I could barely lift the boot lid, let alone the case when I realised that I wasn't expected to. The girl was already calling someone from another room.

"I'll show you your room and Tim will bring your luggage directly. We'll get your car tidied away as well. May I have your keys?"

She came around the end of the desk, holding her hand out and looked to be heading for a doorway behind me. I had to turn to face her the whole time or she'd see the arse ripped out of my suit. A kid appeared at the doorway she was aiming for so I had to do a little dance to keep facing them. The last thing I felt like was dancing.

I finally got into the room on my own about half an hour later. I took my shoes off and lay on the bed. I felt massively relieved for a couple of minutes and then suddenly remembered everything at once. Shit, shit, shit. I reached for the phone then tried to think who I needed to ring first. Carpet for big client out of control, warehouse out of control, wife out of control, my life out of control.

Bugger. Okay, easiest first. I rang the warehouse. No answer. Of course, closed.

Keith was not at home but his mother was:

"I'll take a message for Keith, but I'm not best pleased with you Mr Healey."

"What are you talking about?" Keith rips off my materials and time to give his mother a free carpet and she's not best pleased!

"You can't be going round telling people you've died and then popping up live as Larry, it's just not right. Gave me a real fright."

No doubt she thought she wouldn't get her free carpet finished: "Look, tell Keith to ring me at the Monarch Hotel as soon as you see him." Then realised I could be waiting days: "When do you expect that might be?"

There was a silence and then she said: "Well, I told him his tea would be ready at seven and it's already ten past now."

"Just take this number and get him to call me. As soon as he shows up. Before he has his tea, mind." I emphasised.

While I waited, I thought I would see what clothes Alf had seen fit to pack for me. I stood up gingerly and walked very slowly over to the case on the stand and opened it, praying that he had played the white man.

Of course he hadn't. It contained the grey track suit I had got when I thought I would do some jogging the previous year. At least you could say it was clean, never having been used. Nice of Alf to actually fold it up, I thought. And then saw why, the bastard had given me the Dragon's tracksuit, carefully folded to hide the pink stripe down the seams. Sadistic old shit. Still, no buttons, no belts suited me right then.

I was easing gently into the top, struggling for breath, when Keith rang:

"What are you doing there boss? he said, then chuckled, "You haven't got some piece of skirt have you?"

"Keith, right now I need your attention and help, not your bleeding wisecracks." I took a breath, which was a mistake, and went on: "First off, have there been any messages at the warehouse for me? Second, have there been any visitors?"

"I wouldn't know about messages, I'm not a bleeding secretary, am I? You've had visitors though."

"So who was there?"

"Your missus came in wanting to know about a Roller. I hadn't a clue what she was on about."

"What was she saying?"

"She said if you had a Roller she damn well wanted a part of it and where were you..."

Alf must have gloated to his sister that he'd damaged me and the Roller. That would have perked her up.

"Who else?"

"Well, nobody really but the fitters we've got working on

72

the Freeman job are making noises about wanting their dosh."

"They can bloody well wait till they've finished the work, bloody chancers."

"But they're saying they want the first half by starting time tomorrow, in cash too, or they're pulling off the job!"

Twenty-five fitters working on fifteen hundred each for the job meant I'd need nineteen grand by six the next day. I'd have to go to the bank first thing, pay in the bank draft and get some cash out for the fitters.

For now though, I was hungry and tired. I called down to reception to get some room service.

"I'm sorry Mr Healey, we have no facility for room service other than breakfast and the kitchen is just closing now. If you come down to the bar, we can probably sort out a sandwich for you."

I looked at my watch. It was just after nine.

I found the bar. A barman in a red waistcoat and bow tie was cleaning a glass with a tea towel. There was tinkling piano music very low and a silver-haired couple sitting at a corner table staring into space: "Reception said you could get a sandwich together for me, I'll have a large whiskey as well while I'm at it."

He stopped wiping the glass and stared at me without moving: "I'm sorry Sir, but I can't serve you. We have a dress code."

An enormous anger started boiling inside me: "In the last seventy-two hours," I shouted, "I have had two cars wrecked, two suits wrecked, one marriage wrecked, three ribs broken, been arrested, threatened by City gangsters in suits and I won't even go into the disease I've caught. I'm hungry, I'm tired and I'm getting very close to the edge."

The old couple were all attention with eyes and mouths wide open and heads cocked to one side like dogs. The barman hesitated, then turned slowly to the optics and measured a treble.

He put it down in front of me and pointed to a door at the other end of the room: "I think if Sir would care to move through to the Drawing Room there, I'll see what can be done about a sandwich. Ham, or cheese?"

The drawing room was packed with flowery armchairs and had a tv in the corner showing weird-looking angry women in a field shouting at policemen. Nobody was watching, I was the only person there. I found a chair with a side table, put my drink down and gingerly lowered myself into the seat.

I thought about what I had just said about a wrecked marriage and realised that was probably off the mark if the Dragon had been sniffing around after the Roller. There had to be some way I could use that to make life easier for myself. For now though, I needed to sort out the fitters.

The sandwich arrived in little triangles with cress on the side of the plate, very much a case of chef's gone home. Still, I suppose it was just about edible.

I went to bed mulling over various permutations. I was just dropping off when it hit me. I could have it all, and have some revenge while I was at it. Thinking of the Dragon's face when she realised she wasn't going to get it all her way, I laughed to myself and winced at the same time. I called reception and arranged a morning call. I needed to start early if I was going to stand any chance at all of pulling it off.

Considering my physical condition and the filthy looks my tracksuit generated in the dining room, I felt pretty tip top. A hearty fry-up and a couple of cups of coffee sealed the feeling. I asked for the car to be brought round and headed for the bank. Despite seeing Alf's damage to the passenger side again, the Roller brought a smile to my face as I cruised into town. At least the people on the off-side would be impressed.

I parked and entered the bank with a light step. There was the usual five counters with three manned and I stood there for a minute assessing the different queues. I always avoid the ones that have anyone grasping folders or bulky packages or bags. It can drive you bloody nuts to be stuck behind some-one paying in three hundred pounds in loose change. I took a punt on three people clutching cheque books or paying-in books with nothing else in their hands. It still took twenty minutes to get served, longer than people in the other queues who had come in after me.

"Balance please," I said as I handed over my cheque book. She glanced at the cheque book and said: "Certainly Mr Healey, I'll just be a moment."

She disappeared, coming back a minute later with a frown and a piece of paper. She passed it over the counter. It said: "Balance £12,482.32 O/D

Available £0"

She said: "Mr Wurthers would like a word with you, could you go to the end there and wait. He'll be with you presently."

"What's going on? Why is there nothing available? What's happened to my twenty grand overdraft facility?"

"Mr Wurthers will explain if you just wait a minute."

"He'd better bloody well have a good explanation." She looked awkward and tried to look round me at the bloke behind in the queue who was trying to hand his paying-in book past me to the counter. I gave her what I hoped was a filthy look then turned and gave the evil eye to the pushy bugger behind before moving over to the little coffee table in the corner.

I wondered whether to sit down or stand for maximum outrage but then realised that a tracksuit with pink stripes stripped me of any dignity I might have had. The steel-edged door next to me opened and Wurthers emerged.

"Ah, Mr Healey," he said while looking down his nose. "I've been trying to get hold of you since yesterday afternoon. I left at least four messages."

"What's going on? Why do I have no available funds?" I asked. Fantastic, I thought, you go out of the warehouse for a couple of hours and all hell breaks loose.

He looked up at the corner of the ceiling: "Mr Davidson, your company accountant, felt that the company could not realistically service its debt so requested that the company's bank account be frozen pending calling in the receivers."

I couldn't even find the words to scream at him I was so shocked. Davidson was a boring little jerk at the best of times who couldn't meet your eye even if you were saying something good to him. A charity case.

Hang on, I thought, hadn't I taken him on at Beryl's request? To help out a friend of the family? Oh God, he was a fucking plant! That fucking family! Fucking Alf!

"You stupid bugger," I whispered. "Do you believe everything that anyone tells you? You bloody well don't when it means doing something to help a customer rather than shaft them."

"Mr Healey," he said, looking like I'd just murdered his grandmother. "If you cannot keep a civil tongue in your head I shall have to ask you to leave."

"Oh don't you worry, I'll be leaving. Leaving your fucking useless bank." The rest of the bank had gone quiet, I glanced around and over a dozen sets of eyes all suddenly looked somewhere else. Then I added: "Taking this with me." I opened the bankers draft and let him see the figure on it before I turned with as much dignity as a pink-piped tracksuit allows, and strode out of the place.

I sat in the cocoon of the Roller and tried to work out where to go next. I needed to get cash for the fitters. I wanted to do something terrible to Davidson and I had to get some real clothes. Oh yes, and I should work out which way to handle the Dragon. Injured innocent or go on the offensive. Going on the offensive was tricky, with her bloody brothers so eager for a fight and, like twenty-four hour plumbers, available night and day. Ha, I thought, they should call themselves AAA-Injuries and get a listing in the Yellow Pages. I laughed, and immediately regretted it. Damned ribs.

I looked around through the window glass and saw Thomas Anson & Son, Gentlemen's Outfitters behind on the other side. That settled it, clothes first, then cash. But that wouldn't work, I had no money on me and I daresay Thomas Anson and his son would be a bit pushed to give me change out of a bank draft big enough to buy a house.

I locked the car again and started trying to find a different bank. After ten minutes, I walked into a largish branch of Westons. There was a special counter for enquiries so I went to it and stood behind a lady trying to set up an international transfer to her son in India. I hoped the bank in India worked the transfer quicker than this one, the poor kid would have died of famine otherwise by the time he got it.

Eventually, I got my turn: "Do you have safe deposit boxes?" I asked. The clerk smiled.

"Certainly Sir," he said. "We extend that service to our customers for thirty pounds a year."

"Great," I said. "I'd like to cash this draft and put most of the cash in a box." I showed him the draft.

"Are you a customer of Westons, Sir?"

"No."

"We only extend the safe deposit box service to our customers," he said.

"But I can be a customer as soon as I have the cash."

"So you would like to open an account?"

"I suppose so."

"I'll get you the forms Sir. If you'd care to wait a minute?"

"Hang on," I said. "Is this going to take long?"

"Well Sir, we have to fill out the forms, establish your identity, take a deposit from yourself and then we'll have the account up and running in less than a week."

"So what happens to the deposit until then?"

"Nothing Sir. It will be accessible when the account is operational."

"And when can I have a box?"

"At the very moment the account becomes operational."

"So you're asking me to fill forms for an hour, hand over a large amount of money, which I then cannot get at for a week? Can't I just get cash for the draft and put it in a box?"

"If we have that amount of cash here in the branch we can cash the draft but we will charge a fee. We cannot make a box available until the account is operational." He smiled.

"So where do you expect me to put thirty-three grand of cash in the meantime?" This was getting silly.

"There are independent safe deposit companies other than banks, not that I can recommend any in particular. Bullion Deposit for example over in Stoop Street, or Bankside Security in Harlow." Now we were getting somewhere.

"Right, how much fee do you charge?"

"One per cent," he said. "That is assuming we have that amount on hand."

"Can you check?"

"Certainly," he said, although his smile was looking a bit frosty.

I became aware of someone behind me tapping their foot. I turned, and there were three people behind me looking impatient. I was about to sound off then thought I'd better not attract too much attention to myself. The thought of walking out with thirty-three thousand, three hundred and thirty-three pounds in cash made me nervous. I ignored them and after a few minutes Mr Smiles returned.

"Well, I have bad news and good news," he said. "We can only run to thirty thousand in fifties, the rest we can either do in smaller denominations or issue another draft for the balance."

Now until that moment I hadn't really thought about how big that amount of dosh would be. Of course it would need to be fifties otherwise I'd be filling carrier bags with the stuff. Having the balance as another draft might be useful given my relationship with my bank. It was just as risky as cash but at least a draft is a single piece of paper.

"Fine, fifties and a draft it is," I said. "Have you got a bag I can put it in?"

"It will only be six fat normal letter envelopes," he said.

I gestured at the clothes I was wearing.

"Ah," he smiled. "Not much in the way of pockets there, eh Sir? I'll see if I can rustle something up. If you could just pass me the draft?" He held his hand out for it and I pushed it through.

I got back to the Roller with my fat foolscap envelope, let myself in and locked the doors. Now what?

I looked around the gorgeous cabin to see if there was anywhere I could hide the dough. The glovebox wasn't big enough and there seemed to be motors and stuff under the seats. I tried pulling at the carpet but it was fixed. I was going to have to use the boot although somehow it made me nervous. I sat watching the space around the car, in the mirrors, ahead, to the sides, but nothing seemed weird. I couldn't see anyone that I had seen in the bank so I slipped a few of the notes out of the package and got out and opened the boot. I quickly eased back the carpet and slid the package underneath.

I locked everything up and walked into Anson's. A greasy-looking geezer ducked his head and grimaced at me: "Good morning to you Sir. Is there anything I can help you with?"

"Does it look like there's anything you can't help me with?"

He sort of sniggered: "Well, I was thinking that Sir could possibly benefit from a little spruce up. Perhaps a subtle tweed? Something with a little more structure?" The grimace had become more hideous, I suppose it was some sort of amusement.

"Are you Anson, or Anson's son?" I ventured.

He looked embarrassed: "Ah, well, actually Mr Anson's

son was my father-in-law, I'm actually not an Anson. More of a Smith."

"Oh well," I said, "I assume you know what you're doing. Get me into some proper clothes as soon as possible."

He scooted out from behind the glass-topped counter and looked me up and down: "Hmm, I would imagine that Sir is a forty-two chest, thirty-six waist, inside leg twenty-eight. Is that about the size of it?"

Not exactly flattering, but I have to say he seemed to know what he was doing. He darted over to the rails and started quickly running through hanging suits and jackets, tutting to himself and taking some of them out, laying them over his left arm.

He came back with half a dozen jackets and I have to say, he'd chosen well. I tried a couple I liked the look of. They were a good fit, although it took a while to get into them with Smith holding and me trying to slide in with as little movement as possible. I took two suits, a couple of pairs of casual trousers, five shirts and some y-fronts, wearing one of the suits as I left. I asked him to dispose of the tracksuit, an action that he obviously approved of but was equally repelled by.

I got back to the Roller and there was no sign of anything untoward so I put the clothes in the boot and was reassured by the slightly discernible bulge in the carpet. I pointed the flying lady towards Stoop Street and was conveyed there without drama. It was certainly nice to be sitting above the other traffic, easier to see what was going on.

I'd never really noticed Bullion before even though I'd driven down the street loads of times. It had a yard with a discreet sign and a drive-in entrance. There were no other cars parked which gave me more room to manoeuvre the bulk of the Roller easily, so I took advantage and turned it ready for leaving.

There was a door in the corner of the yard. I wouldn't have dreamed it was the entrance if it hadn't been for a little name-plate on it. It was reassuring that they didn't let me in without a lot of questions over the answer-phone by the door. I noticed that there was a camera on the wall above me. When I finally got through the door I found myself in a short bit of corridor with an even bigger door at the far end. There was a security window on the right and I could see a bloke with a uniform sitting behind it.

There was a squawk of feedback from a loudspeaker above the window and then: "So, Mr Healey, you want to open an account for a security box?" I couldn't see a microphone for me to talk into, so I just talked towards the glass: "That's what I just said outside."

"Yes. Now, do you know what size of box you need Sir?" I didn't want to flash around the large envelope clutched under my armpit inside the new jacket.

"Big enough to hold a few envelopes I suppose."

"Envelopes come in all sorts of shapes and sizes."

"Well, what size boxes do you do?"

"Sixty by two-eighty by four-sixty millimetres is our small-est."

I had no idea what that would look like: "How big is that? Can you show me?"

He sighed and made a couple of motions with his hands

like an angler and then one with his fingers. I visualised the cash and thought it would probably fit.

"Okay, I'll take one of those. How much is that?"

"The smallest boxes are charged annually in advance at sixty-eight pounds fifty."

"Fine," I said, "I'll have it." I reached into my pocket and extracted two notes from the wedge I'd taken into Ansons and slipped them through the slot under the glass.

He spent forever finding the change and writing a receipt. Then he laboriously filled out the membership form, asking me the occasional question. I was thinking about the rest of the day as he did so. All I had to do was leave thirteen grand in the box take the other nineteen to London to pay the fitters and keep them working. I supposed it might be an idea to check that the warehouse staff were still doing what they were paid to do, although paying them might be a bit tricky without a bank account available.

"Right Mr Healey," came the voice from the speaker. "All done now. We'll give you one key for your box, we hold the other. Both are needed to open the box. We recommend that you keep yours in a safe place for obvious reasons. You'll need suitable identification to get access."

Finally, I was buzzed through to the next lobby. There were some seats and coffee tables. A drinks machine in the corner. A counter with proper-height tables each side, running to the corners of the room. Another secure door. A different uniformed geezer was sitting behind the glass screen. He reached down and pulled up a box which he passed through a hatch. I took it to the furthest bit of bench and arranged the thirteen grand in it. It didn't look like much but at least it would be off my hands.

"Are you all done Sir?" he said when I returned to the counter. "Go through the other door when I buzz you, put your box in a slot and lock it there with both keys. Ring the bell and I'll let you out."

I followed all the instructions and was soon heading out into the yard with the large envelope clutched under my jacket. There was a second car in the yard, a Rover. As I looked, a large figure emerged and walked towards me and the door, looking around the yard and up at the surrounding buildings as he moved. As he came closer, we both did double-takes. It was Arthur, Beryl's even worse brother.

I was hoping he wouldn't notice me out of context but I could see the process of recognition in his face. He shook his giant head and blinked hard, then smiled, then frowned, then growled: "George Fucking Healey. I hear you've been a naughty little cunt!"

"Hello Arthur, why are you trying to put me out of business?" I asked. "That's not going to help your darling sister is it?"

He grabbed my lapels and swung me around, till there was a horrible pain in my arse. He had dumped me on the Spirit of Ecstasy, which I can safely say is not a comfortable place to be sitting. In the course of swinging me, I lost my grip on the envelope and it fell to the ground. He didn't spot it immediately and I have to say I prayed that he wouldn't. He was busy pulling his fist back to inflict damage to my person when he stopped, bent to the ground, and picked it up.

"You seem to have dropped this George," he said. "I wonder what little secrets might be lurking in here."

Oh God, I thought, please let him die of a heart attack, right now.

He showed no sign of doing so and let go his remaining hand on my lapel to better open his prize. I slid off the grille of the Roller onto the ground and heard my trousers rip as I did so.

He reached into the envelope and pulled out a five grand band of fifties. He looked at them with a mixture of recognition and puzzlement before looking into the envelope.

"Have you been robbing banks George?" he growled. "Trying to impress the family?"

"Arthur, I'm a businessman. I have to pay people. They don't work just for threats. I need to pay my guys." I could see thought processes clouding his brow.

"Well here's a thing George." Oh shit, he was looking pleased with himself. "I hear you've gone and left my sister in the lurch, and it strikes me as she's probably going to need some working capital to keep things afloat till she sorts out how much you owe her." I closed my eyes and tried to disappear but he went on:

"It seems reasonable to me that you should entrust this cash with me to pass on to Beryl to make sure she don't go hungry in this painful time for her."

My mind was doing mental arithmetic and whatever way I looked at it I was screwed. I think I would have rather suffered a pop on the nose than the grief I was now lumbered with. At least Arthur seemed to have lost interest in me which seemed like a blessing. He turned and headed towards the entrance door of Bullion taking my cash with him.

I sat on the ground and cursed my luck. Why should my brother-out-law be there? Did he have a box too? He had looked like he was casing the place before he saw me. Maybe he looked at every building like that, assessing possibilities and threats. What to do now? I had to pay the fitters by six and they were a good hour away. They needed nineteen grand and change. I had thirteen grand in the box. I had to go back in but there was no way I was going in with Arthur inside and it wouldn't be too clever to be outside when he'd finished whatever he was up to.

I dragged myself into the Roller and drove to the end of the street where I could still see the entrance to Bullion. I parked and hoped to God that he would go the other way. A Rolls is not exactly inconspicuous and I could do without furthering my friendship with the in-laws. I adjusted the mirror so that I could see down the street behind, while I ducked down as low as I could in the seat. I felt around the pain in my arse to see if there was any blood. There was, so I turned sideways to be able to see the seat and there was a great big smear of brown on the tan Connolly.

"Sod it," I shouted. "Shit, damn, bollocky crap, sod it." I was sick of this game. I wanted to just close my eyes and escape but some bloody-minded instinct for survival kicked in and I found myself thinking through various plans of action.

Simple three-way choice: get nineteen grand together, persuade the fitters to take less, or miss out on the biggest, easiest money I had ever made and in the process lose my balls to Franklin B. The third was simply not an option. The second was extremely unlikely and could well end up unintentionally with the third. So that left the first. I was six-and-a-bit grand short and had just four hours to find it.

As I was collecting my thoughts, my mind wandered to the man I was waiting for. Arthur was a grade-one bastard. A long history of bank jobs and extortion interspersed with stretches at Her Majesty's pleasure didn't exactly add up to clever. The idea of him having any surplus anything needing storage in a secure facility was a joke. He blew it all as soon as he got it on dodgy women and dodgy cars. The Rover was proof of that. No doubt he mistakenly thought it had class because it had a bit of wood on the dashboard. His brother Alf was smarter in that respect.

So what was he doing at Bullion? He had to be sizing the place up. First off, I was relieved that I would be getting my remaining money out in a few minutes. Second, and more importantly, how could I take advantage of the situation?

If I shopped my dear brothers-in-law I might as well get myself a coffin right then. It would take a little more thought than that. I needed to find someone who hated them other than the Old Bill. I thought for a while, keeping an eye on the rear-view mirror. I didn't get anywhere and turned my thoughts to the five grand I was short. I considered the possibilities available to me of raising that sort of wedge instantly and although I was trying hard to steer it another way, kept coming back to the Roller. Surely not. Just twenty-four hours after finally getting a Rolls, I was considering selling it and I didn't even know if it would be possible. I didn't hold out much hope, what with the state of it, but it was my only option.

I caught a movement in the mirror, the Rover was easing out of the yard. To my horror it was coming my way. I curled up sideways on the seat as low as I could. I was straining to hear the noise of it passing by. I caught the burble of it approaching but then the noise steadied to an idle. I stopped breathing. A door slammed and I heard footsteps. I nearly crapped myself when I realised I'd forgotten to lock the doors. I nearly passed out when the door opened and Arthur squatted down till his face was almost touching my ear.

"Not feeling too good, eh George?" He said softly.

I tried to speak but nothing came out.

"You're probably best off going home and having a little lie down." He grabbed my hair and twisted my head towards him. Jesus that hurt. Somehow the twisting set off all the pain in my ribs. He continued, "And you won't be running off to the filth with any stories!" He twisted harder. "Will you?"

I shook my head.

"I'm glad we understand each other George, keep it all in the family eh?" He let go of my hair, stood up and returned to his car leaving my door open and departing in a cloud of oil smoke.

I shut the door and tried to slow down my breathing. I suppose I should have been grateful for small bleeding mercies but I have to say I felt a bit effing miffed.

I had to get the rest of the money. It occurred to me that if I hadn't been so worried about losing it I wouldn't have lost it. I think that's poetic justice but I'm not a poet so why should it happen to me?

Once I'd got my breathing back to normal, or as normal as was normal at that time, I tried to work out my order of service so to speak. I had to get the fitters paid or the whole bloody thing was going to go pear-shaped. My trousers were bad but I didn't feel like trying to change in the car. I swung the car around and headed back into the Bullion yard.

I got a few odd looks from the staff that had seen me not forty minutes before, as I arrived with a carrier bag full of clothes but they were passably polite. They directed me to the customer toilet where I gave myself a complete change of clothes and managed to wash most of the blood off in the little basin. I wet the discarded shirt thoroughly and wrung it out before putting it back in the bag within the discarded trousers.

I went through the process of retrieving the rest of the cash and distributing it through the pockets of the discarded jacket. When I was about to leave I asked if one of the staff could accompany me to the car.

"I'm afraid that is a service we only extend to deluxe account holders," he replied. "Of course, if you wish to upgrade your account to deluxe, we can run through the application now." he said, then added: "Sir."

"How much is that going to set me back?"

"Forty pounds per annum," he said.

Sod that I thought. "Look, thanks for nothing, I think I'll

risk it."

That's not to say that I didn't take a long, hard look out into the yard from the inside the last door, to see that there was nobody loitering. Especially nobody related to me by marriage.

I made it to the car and locked the bag containing clothes in the boot, having taken out the wet shirt. Once inside the car I attempted to wipe the blood off the tan leather. Unfortunately, I ended up spreading a paler blood stain over a larger area of seat. I would have been better off continuing over the whole interior and pretending it was meant to be pink.

I chucked the shirt behind the seat and set off for Gilby and Mather. On my way there I saw a stationery shop so I parked and picked up some wages envelopes.

I drove round the back of the dealership to the pre-owned showrooms and was stopped at the entrance.

"Sorry Sir," said the bloke on the gate. "Bodywork repairs are in Fletchling Street."

"I don't want repairs," I said. "I want to return the car. I don't like it any more." Not strictly true of course, but I wasn't as enamoured of it as I had been the previous day.

"I'm sorry Sir, you can't just return a car because you don't like it any more," he said. "Especially as it appears to have been in the wars."

"Look," I said. "I need to speak to someone with some authority."

"Suit yourself," he said huffily. "Wait here and I'll see if there's anyone available." He went back into his hut and got on the phone. I got out and lit a fag. As I waited, I thought how much they might offer me. The modifications Alf had inflicted could surely be put right for a grand or so and the leather cleaned up for half that. So, given that they had to take a bite for their trouble I could surely expect to get fifteen or so.

Eventually the salesman who had sold me the car the day before came out of the building.

"Good afternoon Sir," he said somewhat coolly. "Do I understand that you no longer find the vehicle desirable?"

"Yes," I said. "No, I find it desirable despite the unfortunate damage that has occurred, but my circumstances have changed overnight."

"Ah," he almost gloated. "You have a slight cash-flow imbalance Sir?"

"Something like that," I said between gritted teeth.

"Well, let's see now." He walked around the car, squatted down by the bent panels and ran his fingers over them shaking his head and sucking air through his teeth. As he stood up he looked inside at the front seat and looked like he'd swallowed a lemon. "And the stain is...?" he said with distaste.

"It's blood," I tried to say with dignity. "I cut myself."

He looked appalled but continued around the motor. He came to a stop in front of me.

"Normally, we wouldn't dream of taking a car in these circumstances and in this condition but since you are a customer of sorts and we know the vehicle, we could offer you ten thousand pounds refund on your credit card."

Bloody robbers! Ten grand was just about bearable given my pressing need, but a refund on the card was no bloody use to me at all. The fitters would no more accept a card payment than a hole in the head.

"How about eight grand, cash?" I said.

"No, I'm afraid we could not possibly do that. Even if we carried large amounts of cash on the premises, there are regulations about refunds of card payments you know."

"That's no good to me at all, I'll have to go elsewhere."

He shrugged his shoulders. "That's your prerogative," he said. "Good luck and do bear in mind that my offer is not open beyond this meeting."

I drove away from the cheating bastards at Gilbeys frantically thinking what to do next. The fitters wanted around seven hundred and eighty each in cash but I only had enough for five twenty-five each. If they downed tools without their money I'd still have to pay them for the night they'd already done. Then, I'd only be able to afford to pay nine of them to continue. The job would then take nine nights and the Queen was due to visit the Sullivans building on the Monday, less than five days away. I was fucked unless I could get them to take less.

I needed somewhere discreet to sort out the pay packets so I headed for the warehouse. It took longer than I thought as the Roller needed petrol and it took for-bloody-ever to fill it. I was sure the new litre things went quicker and cost more than the old gallons. Lucky I had the gold card, I couldn't afford to be throwing the cash around.

As I drove into the warehouse staff car park there was a little group of employees watching. When they saw the state of the motor they started sniggering. I got the bag out of the boot and walked towards them.

"What's so bloody funny?" I asked. None of them responded. "Right, get back to work you lot, and less of your bloody lip."

They muttered among themselves and headed back to the

staff entrance. I went up the outside staircase and headed for my office. Maureen stopped me as I passed through her office to get to my own.

"Oh Mr Healey," she said as if I was the answer to all her prayers. "I've been so worried. Where have you been? Could you not phone in? There's so many messages and some of them sound really important. I've not known what to do. Especially the ones from your wife...she sounds rather annoyed. And Keith needs to see you."

I walked past her into my sanctuary and locked the door behind me. I took a deep breath and got down to work putting ten notes into each of twenty-five wages envelopes. Without any smaller notes, I had to hope that five-hundred would be as acceptable as five twenty-five. As I finished and was putting the packs in my pockets there was a pounding at the door.

"Go away Maureen!" I shouted, but Keith's voice came back:

"Hey boss," he shouted through the door. "Have you got the scratch for the fitters? We need to get up to town sharpish else the buggers won't work."

"Okay Keith, let's get going," I said as I opened the door and passed him and Maureen.

Maureen was starting to gabble a list of messages and requests but I left the building with Keith in my wake and Maureen's words fading.

"Bloody Hell Boss," he exclaimed as he saw the car. "Your missus was right about a Roller but what have you done to it?"

"Shut up Keith." I said. "Get in."

He went to the passenger door. "Seems to be locked Boss," he said, pulling on the handle. I guessed that dear Alf's modifications had caused a problem.

"Just get in the back Keith." Then I realised how that would appear. No way was I going to let myself look like a chauffeur.

"Wait up," I said. "I'll get in the back, you drive the thing."

He looked doubtful. "Are you sure? I've never driven anything but the Transit."

"Well it's about the same size, so you should be right at home. And it's only got stop and go. Where's that A to Z you bought last time?"

"Oh right," he said. "I'll get it out the van. Hang on a tick."

It was a good job I'd remembered it as neither of us had a clue where to go once we'd got to London. It was hardly the impression I'd like to have made; being ferried around the city in a Rolls with a cigar in hand and a liveried driver. Scruffy Keith using all the finesse of diesel Transit driver, a bent limo and me scrabbling through the A to Z in the back, peering out up at the street names.

We got there with some time to spare so Keith showed me how they'd been doing so far. It was impressive. The offices where the Wilton had been laid had a hush about them even though there were loads of people working. It all sounded harsher and more clattery on the floors that were not yet done.

"Where do we meet?" I asked Keith.

"I arranged for us to use the canteen until the offices empty for the day," he replied. "It's on the first floor."

We installed ourselves with a cup of tea in a corner of the

canteen. Keith offered me a ciggie but I'd rather smoke my own, something with a bit of class.

He lit up. "Mr Healey..? he started. He was obviously after something. "What's going on?"

"What do you mean? I replied.

"Well, this week has been a bit odd."

"Odd?"

"Yeah. I know this job is a big one and all that, but suddenly you're at the Monarch, your missus is chasing all over to find you, you disappeared off the map yesterday, you turn up with a pranged Roller and it looks to me like you've got something wrong with you."

"How do you mean, wrong?" I said. "I'm not sure it's any of your business."

"Fair enough," he said, "I don't want to pry but I just thought you might be in trouble and I might be able to help."

Now, I have to say this came as a bit of a shock. Generally, everyone I know is out to get something or make problems. Of course there had been Trish being pleasant at the weekend, but that hadn't taken long to turn into trouble.

"Keith," I said. "This job is the biggest thing we've ever done and I could really do with it going right."

"Well yeah, of course Boss. But if you need help with anything else." he trailed off, then suddenly changed gear and said: "Here's the first of the fitters."

The twenty-five fitters appeared in dribs and drabs over the next quarter of an hour. Some got themselves tea, some just sat and waited. When they were all there, I stood and said:

"Well done lads. I've had a look at what you managed to do yesterday and I'm well impressed."

"Where's the money?" one of them said from the back. No manners these days.

"I'm coming to that. I'm so impressed that if you keep it up and finish on Friday night, there'll be a bonus of two-fifty each." If I made anything for myself out of this, it was going to be a bloody miracle what with this leaking money in all directions.

There were some smiles and an approving murmur from them.

"However, that bonus is conditional. The work has to be up to the same standard you've already done." There were some nods. I paused, "And, the up-front payment has to be split over today and tomorrow."

Some heads started shaking but thankfully most didn't.

"You can have five hundred each now, which as we know, is more than payment for yesterday. The rest of the fifty per-cent you'll get tomorrow at this time." I got the wages enve-lopes out and they started forming a queue.

I could see the ones who had been shaking their heads scowling but they could see the way the wind was blowing and took their packets along with the others.

I have to say I was pretty relieved that it had gone down okay. I was looking forward to getting back to the Monarch, having a steak and an early night. After all, I had to get hold of another seven grand by the following evening.

They went about their work and Keith and I headed for the street. As we left, we bumped into Freeman.

"Ah Healey," he said. "Your workers seem to be doing a good job. Will they be finished by Saturday?"

"That's our schedule, Mr Freeman" I said. "But we can always finish off over the weekend if not."

He started shaking his head, looking panicked. "No, no, no, that will not do at all. The cleaners have to do a perfect job on Saturday and the Police need Sunday to secure the building for the Royal Party on Monday."

"Okay," I said. "I'm sure we'll be done by Saturday." Then another thought occurred to me, "And that being the case, will you have a draft for the balance ready?"

"Balance?" he said, "Oh yes, balance. I'm sure we can have something ready for you."

This was sounding good. Just three days to go till things were going to work out.

"Great." I paused. "Oh, Mr Freeman, there's just one other thing."

He looked irritated, "Well, what is it?"

"Can we see Her Majesty on Monday?" I asked.

"You can see her arrive outside like the rest of the public," he snapped. "Her Majesty's time here is precious and only a very few people will get to speak to her."

"Well I wasn't wanting to speak to her," I responded, "I was just hoping to see her."

"Really Mr Healey, we have enough on our plate without trying to get clearance for you to be in the building. It's impossible, and to be honest, you're somewhat peripherally connected. Why should we put ourselves out?"

This got my goat. "Because I will have made your offices

fit for a Queen."

He gave me an odd look, then laughed. "Very good Healey, very droll, ha ha."

We left him and got back to the car.

As Keith drove away from the City, I was giving some thought to various aspects of the day.

"Keith," I said. "What do you know about Davidson?"

"The accountant?" he replied.

"Yes, that Davidson."

"Funny little bloke isn't he?" he said concentrating. "Can't say I've ever given him much thought. Keeps himself to himself"

"Know where he lives?"

"I think he lives over in Radlett. He said that he lived 'convenient to the station' when I asked him once. Doesn't really tell us anything does it?"

"Was he in today?"

"Didn't see him, but that doesn't mean he wasn't."

"I think we need to look up the personnel records when we get back to the warehouse."

We drove on in silence. The car really was virtually silent but I couldn't hear the clock ticking. Another myth exposed, another disappointment.

We swung into the dark yard, lighting up the building as Keith steered us over to the outside stairs that led up to the offices. It was a relief not to be carrying thousands in cash as we stumbled about in the dark. Keith finally got his keys into the door by using his lighter as a torch and let us in. I put some lights on while Keith dealt with the alarm.

I went to Maureen's office to find the files. The cabinets were locked. "Bloody Hell!" I tried to think where we kept the keys. My mind was blank, I had no idea. "Keith!"

"What's up?" he asked as he came into the room.

"Where does Maureen keep the keys?"

"I'm not meant to know that am I?"

"But I bet you do though. Get on with it eh?"

He went to Maureen's desk and felt around underneath behind the drawers. He pulled out a small key which opened the desk. He took out a box of paper clips from the back and tipped most of them into his hand before a little bunch of file drawer keys dropped out.

"Like bloody Fort Knox, isn't it?" I said.

I took the keys from him and went to the drawer which had the personnel records in. I flipped through the files until I found our Mr Davidson. It was empty.

"The bastard" I yelled. "He's done a runner and taken his records with him."

"What made you think of him?" Keith asked.

"The little shit has lit the blue touch paper and is standing clear."

"What kind of firework has he set off?"

"A bloody great Catherine wheel showering shit instead of sparks everywhere," I responded.

"Okay you've lost me there boss. What are you talking about?"

"Look Keith, it's best you don't know for now but if I need you to do something for me in the next couple of days, can you help without asking too many questions?"

"Sure Mr Healey. Like I said earlier."

I locked the cabinet again and Keith returned the various keys to Maureen's hiding places.

We left the warehouse and went our separate ways.

I drove back to the Monarch trying to figure out how to get out from under the grief the Dragon's family had piled onto me. At least it was only eight o' clock so I'd be able to get some grub. I thought that maybe the answer would come to me once I'd eaten and had a drink.

I stopped outside reception and got the bag out of the boot. I went in and gave the receptionist the car keys. "Please tell me you're still serving food." I said.

"Oh yes Mr Healey," she said brightly. "And your wife's waiting for you in the Lounge."

I froze. "I hope I didn't hear you right," I said.

"Mrs Healy, she said."

"How long's she been here?"

"About forty minutes, I arranged a pot of tea for her. She wanted to go to your room but you hadn't said anything so I thought it best..." she trailed off.

I looked around the reception area. I couldn't see anything broken so she can't have been on the warpath. How the hell did she know I was here? The only person who knew was Keith and he was on my side, I thought.

"What did she say when she arrived?" I asked.

"She said she wanted to surprise you with something nice."

"Well, stone me," I said out loud without thinking.

I stood there struggling to figure out what new stick Beryl

might have found to hit me with. I really had had enough of her and her bloody family that week. Then, I thought, there was a slight possibility she might be straight up. We had been in love once upon a time after all. Then again I thought no, I was kidding myself, it would be some new bloody torment.

"I'm going up to my room," I said. "Can you just tell her to piss off?"

"Well really Mr Healey, there's no call for language like that." She looked flustered. "She really is rather persuasive, I'm not sure I can do that."

But I was already halfway out of earshot on the stairs.

I opened the room and entered, and was just putting the still-wearable items from the bag into the wardrobe when there was the sound of footsteps and argument out in the corridor.

"I'm afraid Mr Healey specifically asked not to be disturbed.." I heard the receptionist say just before the door burst open.

"George Healey!" It was the wrong voice. Not the Dragon's. "Why are you trying to avoid me?"

I stood, baffled, as Trish barged into the room looking like a million dollars. Well, at least a hundred grand. The receptionist stood looking apologetic. Trish stood there with a big smile and a wink. I looked from one to the other, still confused.

"It's okay," I said to the receptionist. "I'll take it from here, thanks for trying."

The girl forced an apologetic smile and backed back out

into the corridor, closing the door as she went.

"Trish, what the fuck are you doing here?"

"Well that's not exactly the big welcome is it loverboy?"

"I'd have thought you'd have had the shame to keep a low profile," I said. "Not that I'm not pleased to see you."

She looked perplexed. "Shame?" she said. "What have I got to be ashamed about, consorting with dangerous drivers?"

At that point I snapped: "Thanks to you and your bloody little gift, I've just had the worst week of my life. I've been beaten up, had my dream car ruined, been robbed of nineteen grand and been evicted from my own home by my in-laws. And added to all that, I'm still not feeling a hundred per cent, even with the antibiotics."

"Antibiotics?" she looked puzzled. "Gift? Are you implying that I'm not pure as driven snow, George? A girl could take offence at that sort of accusation."

"I got a dose off you didn't I? Where else can it have come from?"

"Not off me you haven't. Perhaps you need to be putting your thinking cap on and working out what you've been up to. I'm clean as a whistle." she said, "Oh, and that Jag was not exactly a dream car, was it? Classy-ish all right, but not a dream car."

I struggled to work out what she was saying, and I was getting there, slowly. If I hadn't got the clap off Trish then there was only one possibility - Beryl! The fucking Dragon! In more ways than one. That put a whole new light on things. I sat down on the bed shaking my head. I closed my eyes, pressing my temples and tried to think. I spun back over my 'conversation' with Alf. He'd said he'd overheard his dear sister talking to their mother. The stupid bastard hadn't overheard all of it, or Beryl hadn't been telling all of it.

"Ah," she said. "Someone unexpected? Someone above reproach? I tell you George, when it comes to sex, nobody is above reproach. Life would be a lot simpler if people realised it's just a natural impulse."

"All right Trish, spare us the lectures on the philosophy of morality, what the fuck are you doing here?"

"Good Heavens," she said. "There's an delayed echo in this room. I looked you up because I thought you and I could do each other a bit of a favour."

"How could you do me a favour? Come to think of it, how could I do you a favour?" I asked, and went on: "How the hell did you find me anyway?"

"Oh, it was easy to find you," she said. "I remembered you mentioning this place with some fondness so I just tried ringing and asking for you. Hardly Sam Spade stuff."

I was relieved. If that was how she knew I was here then Keith wasn't blabbing to all and sundry.

"Clever girl," I said. "But what's this about favours?"

"Okay the situation is this, you've got a nasty case of drunk driving imminent and I've suddenly got problems proving how I earn a living. The rozzers want to boost their figures and our unfortunate encounter with them at the weekend reminded them of my existence.

It would be somewhat convenient if I happened to have just started a job, perhaps something like a driver for a smart businessman."

I could suddenly see where she was going with this. "So I wasn't driving the other night! They just made that assumption and didn't ask, or breathalyse you!"

"Very good George, now we're getting somewhere," she smiled.

"For a professional driver though, you're pretty bloody hopeless," I laughed. Then winced in pain. Then remembered how hungry I was. I noticed it was eight forty-five.

"How about something to eat, Mrs Healey?"

"That sounds like an excellent idea." she said.

They tried to tell us it was too late to eat again but Trish turned on the charm and we were soon sorted out with a pair of quite decent steaks and a bottle of wine.

"Surely you shouldn't be drinking with the antibiotics?" she said.

"I'll limit myself to a couple of glasses and you can have the rest," I said.

"Okay George, so what's this tale of woe you were trying to blame me for?"

"Er yes. Sorry about that." I looked at her. She smiled.

"Okay, okay, we need to support each other now, what's been happening?"

"It would probably help if I told you that my wife's family are a bunch of villains who studied under the Fergusons."

"Oh God," she exclaimed. "Clive and Sonny?" She looked suitably worried.

"That's the ones." I continued, "After the famous brothers got banged up, the apprentices were falling over themselves to prove how they should be the inheritors of the empire."

"So they took over the shop?" she asked.

"No actually they weren't clever enough. George Tunstall was the heir apparent and he was very quick to chase Alf and Arthur out of his new manor. They went off and found a place where muscle counted more than cunning, although that's not to say they're completely moronic."

"So, how on earth did you end up with them as in-laws?"

"Believe it or not, dancing."

"Dancing seems to get you into all sorts of trouble," she laughed.

"Yeah, ironical ain't it?"

"So this family of moronic thugs are good dancers?"

"Only their little sister, and I knew nothing of her loving family when we met at the dances. She just had that thing."

She tilted her head and raised an eyebrow.

"You know," I jutted my chin. "She could dance, she knew she could dance and wanted you to know it."

"So why have they got it in for you?"

"They never liked that I didn't need them. I was straight and already doing deals, getting it together. Selling stuff. I ended up in carpets because people always need them. Or think they need them. That kind of family hates you if you're straight, you're not in their circle of silence. They haven't got anything on you."

"But she liked you."

"I could dance. We made a great couple. It stood to reason we would end up in bed."

"But why have they got it in for you now especially?"

"Ah, well. Like I did, they think I've given her a dose."

"That makes it interesting, where has she got it from?"

"Fuck knows. The thought that she's getting some joy somewhere almost cheers me up."

"So what have the family been up to then?" she asked.

"Breaking my ribs, breaking my Roller, breaking my

111

company and ripping me off. To be honest I'm surprised to be still in one piece."

"A Roller, George?" she smiled. "Am I driving you round in a Roller?"

"You are, except that dearest Alf kicked half the panels."

"You'd be surprised how easily panels can be popped, as long as they're not creased."

"How would you know?"

"My brother Dave's in the bodywork trade."

"Both of you then?" I said. Somewhat unfair, but it was begging to be said.

"Ha ha George, watch it," she came back.

"So where does he work then? Maybe he could look at it," I said. "Of course, the other problem is I've got to sell it since my other brother-in-law relieved me of nineteen grand earlier. Not to mention the pair of them got my accountant to get the bank to freeze the company account."

"We could go and see what Dave reckons tomorrow if you like," she said like she was working out her appointments for the day.

"Is he any good with blood on leather?"

"That's easy," she said, beaming. "Hydrogen peroxide ought to sort that out. How did you get blood on the seats?"

"I had a rather intimate encounter with the Spirit of Ecstasy during the course of losing all that money."

"Aw sweet. Not having much luck with the girls this week, eh George?"

I suddenly realised I was having as much fun as I'd had at Bob's wedding. Then I remembered that it certainly wasn't going to be going anywhere further that night. I wondered what Trish was expecting to happen after supper.

"I imagine you have to get back somewhere this evening?" I asked. "Come to think of it, how did you get here?"

"I got a taxi here," she said. "But it would look pretty odd if your 'wife' didn't stay with you overnight. Besides, we can get a nice early start if I stay here with you."

"Well, that's a lovely offer, but you know I'm off games at the moment."

"George," she sounded shocked, "I don't think employers are meant to get that sort of fringe benefit from their employees. I could take you to a tribunal."

"As if I haven't got enough grief."

We finished in the dining room and headed upstairs to the room. I gallantly offered her the bed, saying I could sleep on the sofa but she said what with the ribs and all that I should have the bed. Then she said "Fuck it George, I'll sleep with you in the bed but no hanky-panky."

"I have to say, there's nothing further from my mind."

She helped me with my clothes, tenderly making sure she didn't set off any of the pains. She even hung things up properly.

"You'd make someone a fabulous wife," I said.

"Ha ha, no. I've never been tempted. I like to be in control of my life, not doing someone else's bidding while they sod off fishing." She took her dress off and hung that up, wearing just a slip. She was gorgeous. I looked at her longingly.

"Put your tongue back in your mouth, we've got to get our

113

beauty sleep. At least I have, I think you're too far gone for that to be relevant."

I lay there in the bed with my various aches and pains, and a massive hard-on. Talk about mixed feelings!

She turned away from me in the bed, breathing slowly and I lay there mulling over what a weird week it had been. I kept trying to figure out a way to get my money back from Beryl's family because if there was any way I could keep the car and this chauffeur, I wanted it more than anything. Eventually I drifted off to sleep without really sorting anything out.

I awoke with the same hard-on I had gone to sleep with and alone. I could hear noises from the bathroom so I set about making a couple of cups of tea from the bits and pieces on the chest. There was only that horrible long-life milk but it was better than nothing. Just.

I was nursing mine when she came out of the bathroom in a white robe rubbing her hair with a towel.

"Mouth closed George," she said. "This one mine is it?" then continued, "I suggest you take a turn cleaning whatever you can clean while I get myself dressed. Perhaps you should clean your thoughts while you're at it."

"Have you got anything to put on?"

"Of course, a working girl always has a spare pair of knickers in her bag. Why, were you going to offer me some of your y-fronts?"

"I think I'm going to have to get you a uniform with a hat," I said as I went into the bathroom.

I managed to get passably washed and Trish helped me get

my clothes on. She was relieved that a different girl was on reception as we passed. We had a superb full English and I got them to bring the car around. The bashed side was facing us as it drew to a halt. Trish ran her hands over the dents. "There's nothing there that can't be fixed in a couple of hours," she said. "Let's get going and see Dave."

"How far away is that?" I asked.

"Only about thirty minutes. Over at Radlett," she said.

"Let's get to it then." I went to get into the drivers seat but she followed me.

"Shove over then, if I'm your driver, that's what I'd better do."

I grudgingly moved across to the passenger seat and gave her the keys. She took a few seconds to get comfortable and adjust mirrors and we took off to Radlett.

She drove well, so after a bit I returned to my thoughts about the seven grand or so that I was short for that evening. If only I could get at my overdraft facility at the bank, that would be enough. I needed to get hold of Mr Davidson and persuade him the error of his ways. Somehow get him to persuade the bank to unfreeze the account. Trouble was, if the family had got at him it was going to be bloody difficult to get him to change his mind. I didn't even know where he was, but co-incidentally, we were heading for Radlett.

"Penny for them," she spoke next to me.

"Hmm, trying to work out how to persuade a little rat to undo something the family have made him do."

"And where is this little rat?" she said.

"All we know is that he's in Radlett, somewhere near the station."

"Have you tried looking in the phone book?"

"Now there's a thought," I said. "You're a bit bloody clever for a bird aren't you?"

She gave me a long-suffering look. "I'll find a phone box," she said.

She spotted one in a lay-by we were approaching and left the road with somewhat more grace than I'd managed a few days before. Miracle of miracles, it actually had a phone book in it. I flipped through looking for Davidsons. There were a good few.

"What's his initial?" Trish said behind me, looking over my shoulder.

"I haven't a clue," I said. "He's not exactly a pal of mine."

"Okay, let me see," she said. I moved aside. "No, I don't recognise any of these streets. We'll have to ask Dave when we get there."

"Why don't we take the page?"

"Don't be silly, Dave will have a directory."

"Oh, right," I said, feeling stupid. "Of course he will."

There was a pause and then she asked, "What's he done then, this Davidson?"

We continued on and after a while Trish steered the Roller into a dodgy-looking street of workshops. I was a bit concerned that it wasn't the best place to be with a decent motor but then we pulled up outside a place with a bunch of cars in all kinds of states.

Trish got out and a bloke looked up from the front wing of the Audi Quattro he was sanding and a huge grin split his dirty face.

"Sis!," he shouted. "You won the pools or something?"

"Hi Dave, no. New job I've got, driving Mr Healey around."

He got up and gave her a brief hug before walking approvingly round the car.

When he got round the nearside he stopped and said: "Are you sure you're qualified?" Then added, "Does Mr Healey know you've done this?"

This while I was sitting there in the nearside seat not four feet away from him.

She laughed, "No, George likes mixing with odd people." Then to me, "Come on out George and say hello to my little brother Dave."

I shuffled across the front seats and got out slowly. The acrobatics were doing me in.

I'm not sure about 'little' brother. The man was a hairy giant. He put out his dirty paw and I shook it then looked around for somewhere I could wipe off the sweaty dust he'd just wiped onto my hand. There wasn't anywhere so I just clenched and unclenched my hand hoping it would dry.

"Pleased to meet you," I said looking up at him. "And I'd be even more pleased if you told me this was fixable."

"Piece of piss," he said. "I could have it looking almost as good as new in a couple of hours."

"Got some hydrogen peroxide too?"

He turned around and looked inside, catching sight of the stain on the front seat.

"Ouch, I'm not going to ask what you've been up to. I'm sure we can sort that out too as long as I can raise Big John on the phone."

"Talking of phones," piped up Trish. "Can we ask you about some addresses in the phone book, if you've got one?"

"'Course Sis, you know where the office is."

Trish went off to get the phone book. I was busy wondering what size someone called Big John could be as I looked at the size of Dave.

"How much is that going to set me back," I asked Dave.

"Cost you a couple of ton plus a couple of ponies for Big

John's magic if I can get hold of him."

"Any chance that couple of hours could start right now?"

"What's the hurry?"

"I need to have the option of selling it by the end of the day."

"That would be a shame." He paused for thought. "I suppose Trish would be out of a proper job again if that happened?"

I scanned his face to see if he knew what she did normally but he was completely deadpan.

"Yes, that could be it," I said, as straight as I could.

Trish came out with the book. "Know which of these is close to the station Dave?"

He ran his finger down the list of Davidsons. "No, no, no, no, no, not far Coopers Cottages, no, no, no, aha, Watling Lane, that's probably closest. Why do you need him?"

"I need to get him to realign his loyalties."

"Is that something you're able to do?" he asked pleasantly, looking down at me.

To be honest, I hadn't really thought it all through. Even if I got to speak to Davidson, how would I get him to retract his stupid statement to the bank? And yet again, even if he did, would the bank play ball?"

"I've no idea but I've got to give it a try," I said.

"Strikes me you've either got to frighten him or bribe him," he said. "Now if I came with you that might well frighten him but you want me here popping these panels and rounding up Big John, don't you?"

"Yeah, of course."

"Well you'd better work out what kind of bribe is going to work then."

He had a point.

Trish was standing there smoking a cig.

"Trish," I said, hoping not to sound too see-through. "Coming with me to meet Davidson W.S. of Watling Lane?"

"Sure, if you want company, looks like Dave's busy anyway." Dave had gone inside to the phone.

Trish went and asked the lad who was standing around doing nothing how to get to Watling Lane.

"Simple," she said as she came back to me. "Ten minutes walk that way," she pointed.

We set off walking and I started thinking how pleasant it was to be with someone who was not looking to give me a hard time about every damned thing. She broke the silence only to say, "This way" and "Right, here."

"Trish," I said, "I've just had an idea."

"What's that?"

"If I go to the door he'll recognise me and may not even open up. If I wait down the street here, I can see what's going on at his door without being visible."

"So you want me to get him to open up?"

"It's more likely you can than me."

"And then what?"

"Give me a wave, be a bit subtle, and I'll come along and join the conversation."

"Okay, but make sure you're watching."

She went to the door while I lurked next to a hedge along the street. I could see her ring the bell and wait. Nothing happened. She rang again and eventually someone I couldn't see opened the door. She started talking to whoever it was while I watched for a sign. A sign that didn't come. After talking for about a couple of minutes I saw the door open wider and Trish went in. The door closed.

That had me foxed. Now I was lurking by someone's hedge on a quiet residential street in the middle of the day and beginning to sense curtains twitching. I strolled up and down a bit looking at the front gardens, making approving nods and trying to look like the judge of Britain in Bloom, or at least one of the heats. I could see a little shop on the corner so I walked down to that.

They had newspapers and sweets so I got a chocolate bar and an Express. I stood outside the shop keeping half an eye on Davidson's house down the street while I flipped through the paper. It was all lesbians, protests and triumphal City deals. I didn't understand much of it so sort of skimmed through the other pages while I ate one half of the Twix. Apparently, England were due to play Norway. I didn't even know they played football in Norway. At least England could win that.

I was not getting what was funny about the Gambols as per usual when there was movement up the road. Trish was saying a friendly goodbye to someone on the doorstep with lots of smiling and laughing. As she got back on the pavement she looked one way then the other, caught sight of me and joined me by the shop.

"What the fuck was all that about then?" I asked, bemused.

"Poor little Mr Davidson, William that is, he's a sweetie." She reached out and took the remaining half of the Twix. "I see you've bought lunch then George, last of the big spenders eh?"

"Hang on, hang on," I said. "What about Davidson?"

"He's terrified. That's why he's hiding at home."

"So how did you get in?"

"I pretended I was from the bank, told him there were some bits of paperwork we needed to tidy up."

"And he let you in without thinking that the bank wouldn't have a clue where he lives?"

"I don't know if you've noticed, George, but a smile goes a long way."

Now that was definitely the case with Trish. "So what happened?"

Oh, I made nice noises about his cat, despite the smell, and admired his annuals and then explained how actually I was representing you and not the bank. I asked him what cosh he was under with the charmless brothers and it all came out."

"What came out?"

"It seems our meek and mild William likes to play the tables and this has led him into bad company at times."

"So how much is he into them for?"

"Only five thou, but he seems to be unable to do anything about it," she said. "He's like a poor little bunny rabbit stuck in the headlights."

"So what did you say?"

"I told him that you were having a certain amount of trouble with the boys yourself, and it wasn't helping anything by playing silly buggers with the bank. I said you'd come back with me and have a little chat about how it could all be resolved without any nastiness."

"I'll stick his head in a mangle, the little shit."

"Now that's exactly what you won't do. Come back and be nice. It's the only way out of this."

I have to say it took some doing being pleasant to William Davidson. He really was a miserable little fucker. I managed, thanks to some overdone smiles from Trish every time I was veering towards anger. Anyhow, the upshot was that he rang the bank and explained how he was completely mistaken in his previous view and he had not known about the enormous contract that had just come in and he was very sorry to have inconvenienced them and everything was hunky dory.

Of course it had come at a price. I had to say I would pay off the boys for him and give him shelter at the Monarch until everything was worked out. The bank wanted him to go there in person and that suited me too as I needed to get the cash from the overdraft facility. The only remaining problem was the cat.

"Can't you leave Dennis with the neighbours, or at least get them to feed him?" Trish asked.

He looked glum. "They all hate him because of what he does in their gardens."

I wasn't surprised. Dennis looked like an evil bugger but we were going to have to do something that would keep William happy.

"Well I guess we're going to have to take him with us," I said. I was sure the Monarch would have a fit if we tried to have a cat staying there but I thought we could accidentally 'lose' him after we got hold of the money. "I seriously hope you've got some sort of carrier because there's no way I'm letting him sharpen his claws on my Connolly."

Davidson went off to get his pet cage from his shed. I turned to Trish. "It's going to be daft three of us and the bloody cat walking back to your brother's. Can you stay here and keep him sweet while I nip back for the car?"

"Why don't I go back and get the car. I am your driver after all," she countered.

"Because Dave needs to be paid and I need to inspect his work."

"That's okay. Dave'll trust me to fetch you and take you back to pay him."

"Hmm," I said. "Neither of us want to be left with William do we?"

So we ended up a bad-tempered motley group walking back to Dave's body shop with Dennis the fucking Menace kicking up seven shades of shit in the box, howling like his nuts were stuck in a catflap.

Dave laughed as he caught sight of us and ambled towards us wiping his hands on a dirty cloth. "Well, well, I loved that film The Incredible Journey. You're looking like the final scene!"

His good humour was met with silence. As we watched, a small, rat-faced man got out of the front of the Rolls.

"Hey George, meet Big John, one of the finest interiors men in the business."

"What do you mean *one* of the finest?" came a gruff voice from the little guy. "Is this the vandal who's determined to write off this fine car?"

"Yeah, I'm sorry about that," I said to him. "None of it intentional."

"So what the hell's that?" he said, pointing at the cat cage. "Tell me you're not intending to put that in the car."

"Well, yes we have to. Can't put him in the boot after all," I said. Then added quietly, "More's the pity."

"Him?" said John, "Him? Cat's piss is bad enough on leather but tom spray is just about the worst. Stinks. Do you have any idea how complicated it is to remove?"

I looked at Dave, he grinned broadly. "I think what might be called for here, is a bit of cage customisation."

"What the hell are you talking about?"

Big John chipped in: "Those stinky bastards can spray upwards as well as sideways and down. We've got to contain that fucker, the cage is no good on its own." He looked pointedly at Dave, "You could weld up a box for the cage to go inside."

"And then there'd be nice sharp edges ripping the leather instead of just stinking it up."

I could see this was going to go on all day. "Look, are you finished with the panels and the seat?" I asked them.

"Give us a chance mate, we've only had a hour on it," said Dave. "You do want it looking good don't you?"

Great, I thought. An hour to kill in the middle of nowhere with the most boring man in the world and his psychotic cat.

"Look," I said. "It's really important that we go and do a bit of business in Harlow. Have you got a courtesy car we could use?"

Dave and Big John looked at each other and burst out

laughing. "We haven't got our main dealership accreditation yet, so no," Dave said.

"You have no vehicle at all that we could borrow for an hour or so?" I pleaded.

"Well, I suppose you could use the parts car but there's no way you're having that cat in it."

"Great, "I said. "That's much appreciated. Where is it?"

"Round the back, I'll just get you the keys." He ambled off into the dark interior of the workshop. There was a corner with a couple of plywood walls decorated with girlie calendars and hub caps.

He reached in and unhooked some keys from a board. Coming back, he tossed the keys to me. I didn't catch them needless to say. Picking them up I registered the British Leyland logo on the key fob. Not the classiest ride then, I thought. We left Dennis in his cage in the the shade of the workshop where he seemed determined to chew his way through the metal and escape.

Trish, Davidson and I walked around the back to find a puke-yellow Marina with rusty sills and a broken rear light.

I tossed the keys to Trish, who caught them first time, "You've been telling me you're my driver. Go to it girl."

"Yes'm boss," she responded, touching an imaginary hat with a forefinger.

I have to say, I'd thought Keith's van was disgusting but this was worse. I think the cat could have improved it. There was a film of grease over everything and I thought to myself it was lucky I'd got a spare suit from Ansons.

It took a while to start and when it finally got going the

127

exhaust was blowing, making a foul noise like a cross between a tractor and a cow. Trish did her best but there was no way on earth you could say it was a pleasant journey. Davidson was sat in the back behind me so my view was Trish's profile. A definite result. The Marina ground its way towards Harlow barely faster than a bus. After about fifteen minutes Trish pulled it over to the side of the road with smoke belching out of the engine.

"Oh great," I said. "It's on fire!"

"Don't be silly," she responded. "That's not smoke, that's steam. The fan belt's probably gone."

She reached under the dashboard and fiddled around, eventually finding something that clicked the bonnet open. She got out and I followed. She passed me the keys and said, "Open the boot George and see if there's any cloths in there, water too. This thing might make a habit of overheating."

There was a t-shirt in there but no water. I gave her the t-shirt. She held it up, it was a hideous black thing with red sleeves and a union jack. She immediately started ripping it half. "Serves him right for liking Elton John," she said. She used it to release the cap that held the water in. Steam went everywhere but she calmly poked around in the other bits of the engine.

"Yup," she said. "Fan belt's gone."

"So what do we do now?" I said. "Take a bus?"

"Well I'm sure you don't want to be carrying a load of cash around on a bus, so we'd better just get this going again."

"How do we do that, call the AA?"

"I somehow doubt Dave would pay for the AA. Have you

not heard of tights?"

"What, like on your legs?"

"Yes, George. I'm going to have to whip mine off and we're going to need some water." She went round to the back door of the car and opened it. "William," she said to Davidson. "I'm going to want the back of the car and a moment's privacy, so be a darling and scrounge some water from one of those houses over there."

Davidson seemed delighted to do her bidding and while he was gone, she slipped into the back seat and slid off her tights. It gave me a horny deja whatnot.

"Mouth closed again please George," she said as she returned to the oily engine.

She tore the tights in two and threaded them round some bits of engine before tying a knot.

"Now, where's that William got to?" she said.

We rolled into Harlow even slower than we'd been going before the fan belt broke. Trish thought it best not to overcook the old wreck. We parked up in the multi-storey and made our way to the bank. Mister bloody Wurthers made us wait for about twenty minutes before grudgingly letting us into an interview room. He looked a bit askance when Trish went in with us but she gave him the full hundred-watt smile and he suddenly got helpful and offered us a cup of tea.

We accepted and he went off to get some.

"Can I take you with me everywhere?" I said quietly to her.

She turned the full hundred watts onto me and shook her head, "I'm not sure you could afford that George."

Davidson gave us an odd look then went back to looking at the yacht on the calendar on the wall.

"Well, here we are," said Wurthers on his return, putting a tray on the desk. "Shall I be mother?" he said to Trish, ignoring me and Davidson.

"It's all right Mr Wurthers," she said, "I'll do that. You have things to sort out with Mister Healey don't you?"

The upshot was that after another half hour, everything was back on track and I had a big envelope containing twenty-five bundles of cash with a rubber band round each. Wurthers had been a bit concerned that the company was getting somewhat close to the limit and having heard about the City contract, increased the facility to thirty grand.

When we got back to the car park, I looked at the Marina and thought what would happen if it ditched us on the way back.

"I think we should get a taxi back." I said.

Well, we can't leave this here," said Trish. "It would keep clocking up charges for days before Dave got round to retrieving it."

I had an idea. "We could get a taxi and drive in convoy."

"Not such a bad idea George," said Trish. "Your turn to drive the wreck."

I shook my head, "Not on your life," I waved the envelope. "I'm the VIP here."

Trish turned her smile on Davidson. "William, can you drive the Marina back for us?"

Davidson looked pleased to say "I don't drive, I never learned."

Trish looked daggers at him, looked to me, then back to him, "Right, well you buggers can share the cab, I'll whip this donkey home. I saw a taxi rank just down the street. Let's get this show on the road."

The taxi driver thought it was hilarious when I said, "Follow that car", pointing to the Marina.

"You could follow that just as easily on foot," he laughed.

"Yeah, all right, very funny. Just get on with it."

We hadn't got more than halfway back when, needless to say, the Marina pulled over to the side of the road. I told the taxi driver to pull in behind and got out to see what was up, taking the envelope with me. Trish was out of the Marina and walking towards the cab.

"Run out of petrol, would you believe?" she cast her eyes heavenward. "I'd noticed it registering empty when we started out but I thought it just wasn't working like the rest of the dials."

"Oh well, good riddance and all that." I asked the driver how we'd describe where it was and we continued on to Radlett.

Dave was less than delighted but not terribly surprised to see us arrive in the taxi.

"What have you done with Morry?" he said looking at Trish. "She's far too fragile to be left out alone."

"You're not kidding, she's cost me a perfectly good pair of tights."

"Oh, I'm glad you remembered that trick," he said, looking proud. "Didn't work though?"

"It worked fine but no car works without petrol."

She gave him a withering look and told him where to find the car.

"Well there's no point putting a load of fuel in something that might die any moment."

"Okay, never mind," she said. "Is the Rolls done?"

"Not only is the Rolls done, both panels and seat," he beamed. "But we've also put together a Dennis containment box!"

He dived into the workshop and returned with something that looked like a school woodwork project, only not the sort they'd be showing on open day.

"We'll just put a blanket underneath to protect the leather

from splinters. It should work a treat."

"Well, let's hope so," I said. "Otherwise Big John's worst nightmare will come true." I pulled two-fifty from my wallet and held it out to him. "How much for the box?"

"Don't worry about that, you don't want a receipt do you?"

I saw Davidson wince out of the corner of my eye as I said, "No, that's fine."

"Tell you what," said Dave. "You could do me a favour and take me back to where you left Morry."

"Not dressed like that I can't," I said, pointing to his greasy overalls.

"It's all right, I'll take these off and use them to wrap the petrol can in the boot. Hold on, I'll just grab a fan belt and some juice."

It took a good ten minutes of fannying around but eventually Trish guided the Roller back to the main road with me in the front and Davidson, his bloody cat and Dave in the back. I'm surprised the cat hadn't pegged out from exhaustion what with the noise it was making. It was odd, it felt like a family. Weird, and all forced together in a car.

We came across the Marina and Dave left us, cooing and clucking around his Morry and making remarks like somehow we'd abused it. Bloody idiot. Trish turned to me and said: "Where to George?"

It was mid-afternoon. There was no point in going to the City yet. It made sense to get rid of Davidson and his bloody animal.

"Back to the Monarch," I said. "We'll get William checked in and then head for McCains."

If it hadn't been for the constant screeching of the cat, I would have really enjoyed that journey. Well, I suppose if it hadn't been for Davidson too, but having Trish driving the Roller, with it looking all Kosher too, was magic. I was revelling in it with no idea what might be about to happen.

Needless to say, they weren't keen on Dennis as a guest at the Monarch. Actually, they outright banned him from the premises. However, we got Davidson in. Thankfully they had some cheaper rooms available. I have to say I was going off Davidson in a big way since we had talked the bank around. I couldn't for the life of me think why I had said I would put him up and put up with his cat as well. I told him to sit put, stay shtum and not create any trouble. He was somewhat concerned about Dennis but I told him that Trish would be taking care of the obnoxious beast overnight.

I told Trish about this arrangement as she drove towards McCains.

"You must be fucking joking," was her initial response. After she'd had time to think about it for a while she said: "No really, you really must be fucking joking."

"Listen Trish," I said. "You don't need to feel responsible. If the damned thing got run over or met some other grisly end, I wouldn't care. You wouldn't care. No one would care."

"William would care," she said.

"I don't need William effing Davidson any more. Thanks to you I've got what I needed from him. He's redundant. I don't give a toss what he thinks."

"That's a bit heartless isn't it?" she said.

"What's heartless got to do with it? I'm just sick to death of pussy-footing around other people and doing whatever they want."

She went quiet. I thought about the job, the warehouse, the Dragon and the Dragon's family. A constant flow of other people's agendas that I had to satisfy. I was sick of it. I wanted to have my own agenda.

Trish broke the silence, "Do you think this fuel gauge is accurate?"

"Pull into the services up here, we probably need petrol again, the way this thing guzzles it."

The cat continued his ridiculous song and dance. It was really getting on my tits. We pulled in to the services. "Go to the air line over by the trees," I said.

"The tyres don't feel bad," she said. But she did as I asked.

"I'm sure the tyres are fine," I said as I got out and opened the back door. "It's my ears that need seeing to."

I took the box out and placed it on the ground, shielded from anyone's gaze by the car. I opened the top, reached in and grabbed the little sod by the scruff of the neck. As I lifted him out he sprayed over my jacket and shirt. I had been going to place him on the ground but after that I threw him wailing into the trees. He landed on his feet like they always do and sauntered off into the woods without a backward glance.

"That's not going to put you top of William's Christmas list," she said. Then as I got back in the car, "Oh God George, that is repulsive. You've got to take those off."

"Oh great, and what do you propose I wear?"

"We'll find something but you've got to get those off."

135

"If I take them off they're still going to stink the car up."

"All right George, take them off and I'll go to the ladies and rinse them through."

"But I'll be standing here half naked!"

"Just sit low in the seat, I'll be back in a minute or two."

"We'll have to go back to the hotel. I'm not turning up at McCains bare-chested."

"Have we got time?"

"We're just going to have to."

We got back to the Monarch with me wrapped in Dave's blanket and sneaked back to the room with my damp clothes and precious envelope clasped to my chest. I went to the bathroom and gave myself a quick wash before getting my other suit and a new shirt on. Trish had made a cuppa so we got that down us quickly before returning to the car. As we walked towards the car I saw someone poking about inside.

"Bloody Hell, someone's turning us over," I said, running towards the bugger.

He was leaning into the rear of the car with his back towards us so I grabbed his collar and hauled him out.

"What the fuck are you doing?" I shouted, then saw that it was Davidson. He looked petrified. Trish joined us.

"Where's Dennis?" he said. "What have you done with him?" He looked increasingly desperate, "You've got rid of him, haven't you? You bastard!"

"Steady on William," Trish cut in. "It's all right, we found somewhere nice for him to stay. He'll be fine. Very comfortable in fact."

"I don't believe you," he spluttered. "You never did like

136

him."

"It's all right, he'll be happy where he is," I said.

"You've killed him haven't you!," he screeched as he started raining blows on me. I put up my arms to shield my face but he carried on.

"Now, now," said Trish consolingly. "It's okay. He's fine. He's just gone on a bit of an adventure."

He carried on hitting my forearms but turned to Trish. "You're just as bad, with your smiles and 'William this' and 'William that'. At least he's honest about not liking me."

He was running out of steam now, getting calmer, but his eyes narrowed. "I'm going to get you for this," he hissed.

"Empty threats," I said. "You can't touch me now Davidson."

"We'll see about that," he said as he retreated to the building.

We watched him go and then got in the car.

"You all right?" she said to me.

"Yeah, fine. Let's get going to the City."

"Is there anything more he can do?"

"Don't think so, except prepare his own P45," I laughed.

She drove out onto the road, "Hmm, that reminds me, what are my salary and benefits?"

"Ha ha, you're still on probation girl."

"Well I suppose I'd better make sure I don't put a foot wrong then."

We settled into silence. After a while I said, "Trish, can I ask you something?"

She glanced sideways at me. "As long as you're not going to

ask how a nice girl like me ended up doing what I do."

"Ah." I looked out at the passing signs.

"That was it, wasn't it?"

"Well yeah, actually." I glanced at her. She was looking irritated.

There was a long silence. The signs said twenty miles to London. I was kicking myself for ruining the mood.

"Do you think I don't get asked that on every job I do?" she said. "Does everybody you meet ask you why you ending up flogging carpets? Do you think I don't get sick of it?"

"So what do you say?"

"I tell them history costs extra. A lot extra."

Fifteen miles to London.

Ten miles to London.

"I was doing crappy secretarial jobs where the boss always thought he had the right to feel you up. Getting groped all the time sets you edge. One day, my mate Laura asked me to help her out on a double date. It was a great evening. I had fun, earned more than a couple of weeks' wages and it wasn't as degrading as what went on in the office.

"Laura came up with a couple more dates and it wasn't long before I gave in my notice. Escort work is much the same as going on dates except that instead of getting laid for just dinner and drinks, you're getting paid as well. Everyone knows where they stand too.

"Some guys are really sweet. Widowers who just want some female company Bookworms who want to look big and learn a thing or two. Believe it or not, some do actually just want an escort for a formal dinner or something like that."

"Isn't it worrying not knowing what kind of bloke a client will turn out to be?" I said.

"No more than on some regular dates I've heard about. Of course, you get the odd bastard but you kind of learn how to deal with them. Seems to me George, you get more grief with your relatives than I ever do in my work."

"I'm glad for your sake you haven't happened across them," I said.

"At this rate, I'm sure I will."

That was a worrying thought. Now it was my turn to go silent.

We got to McCaines just in time to pay the fitters and keep them happily beavering away on the job.

I sought out Freeman.

"Oh hello Healey," he said. "No problems with the schedule I hope?"

"No Mr Freeman, should be finished a few hours early tomorrow night. No trouble with the boys I hope?"

"No, no, splendid work, very satisfactory."

"So no problem with a draft on Saturday morning then?"

"Hmm, what? Oh yes, yes of course."

"And no change on the front-row seats for the Queen?"

He looked totally confused, then shook his head, "You can keep asking Healey, but the answer remains a steadfast no."

We drove back North. Trish wanted to go to her place to sort out her clothes and do her hair so she dropped me at the hotel and took the Roller on. We arranged that she would pick me up in the morning to go to the warehouse. I was doubtful about her taking it on her own. It was still bothering me as I ate and then some more as I went to bed.

I dreamed that Trish went out with her friend Laura in the Roller, got pissed and wrote it off. It was a relief when I woke up but I was somewhat disappointed that I hadn't had a horny dream about her. It felt like I wanted to have horny dreams about her all the time.

I had a lonely breakfast and hung around waiting for my lift. As it got later and I had more coffee, I began to think that perhaps my dream was a premonition. That was all I needed, just when everything was coming together. I started kicking myself for letting the Roller out of my sight. I was just beginning to despair of ever seeing car or girl again when the Rolls came into view through the hotel windows making its stately way up the drive.

I played it cool and didn't rush outside but just carefully scanned the bodywork as it went around the circle of grass outside the front door. I saw that no, there was no damage at all. What a relief that was. I went outside and could hardly believe my eyes. She was getting out of the car wearing a smart grey trouser suit with her hair done up in a bun. I didn't prefer the hair that way but by Christ she looked the business. She stood there po-faced, looking for all the world like she was born to it.

As I walked across to her she moved to open the back door. She closed the door after me and got into the front.

"Bloody Nora girl, that's impressive," I laughed.

"I thought I'd better take my probation seriously," she responded with a smile that cracked the facade.

"Impressive," I repeated. "But where's the hat and gloves?"

"The days of liveried servants are over George. I am your employee not your chattel. I don't mind looking smart but I'm buggered if I'm going to put on fancy dress."

"Right, to the warehouse James, and don't spare the horses," I said, as a vision of Trish being buggered passed through my mind.

"You'd better tell me where it is then," she said.

"Oh yes, you've never been to your place of work have you? Head for Harlow and I'll guide you from there."

We pulled into the yard about half an hour later and I guided her to a place that I thought the vans wouldn't need to be loading, turning or otherwise being a bloody menace.

"Right, we'd better introduce you to Maureen, come on up."

Maureen, it turned out, was in a bit of a tizz. "Mr Healey, there you are, where on earth have you been? There's so many messages for you. Have you spoken to Mrs Healey?"

"Hello Maureen," I said, "I'm sure you're handling everything with your usual efficiency. This is Trish, she's doing some driving for me while I recover from these broken ribs."

"Oh Mr Healey, I didn't realise you'd broken your ribs in the accident. You poor thing, are you in pain?"

It was just too complicated to explain the real story so I let her think that the ribs were connected to the damaged Jag.

"I'm okay Maureen, but we need to get Trish on the books, as of last week, say Monday. Can you deal with that? I don't think we'll be seeing Mr Davidson any time soon."

"Right Mr Healey. Have you spoken to your wife? She seems to be very alarmed that she hasn't seen you for days. She keeps calling and quite honestly I just don't know what to say to her any more."

"Okay, okay, Maureen, I'll deal with my wife when it suits me. Just tell her you haven't seen me."

I went into my office and sat down with a sigh of relief, although I realised I was going to have to do something about the Dragon. It was an interesting thought. Did she realise the dose was hers? I went to the window and looked down at the yard. My empire. I could see the Roller shining in the corner. A couple of Transits looking a bit worse for wear. It was odd, in the past this view had turned me on, made me feel worth something, made me proud. Now I was looking at it and seeing what it really was, a grubby carpet warehouse with a grubby yard.

As I looked out, there was movement. A BMW was edging into the shabby space. It looked familiar, it looked like the Dragon's car. It was the Dragon's car! She parked and got out, walking over to the Roller and looking it over before heading for the stairs. She had a face like fury as she mounted them towards the offices.

I could hear her progress as she swept everyone out of her way. I heard Maureen say "Oh, Mrs Healey, I was about to ring..." as Beryl charged past her and threw my office door open.

"George Bloody Healey, where the hell have you been and why has my cheque bounced?" she shouted. I could smell that bloody Caleche perfume.

"Hello Beryl," I said, turning from the window. "How are you, and how's your family?"

"What!, What!" she looked perplexed. "What the fuck are you on about George?" waving a letter at me.

"Well, more specifically, how are my dear brothers-in-law?"

"How the fuck would I know how my brothers are? I haven't seen them for weeks. What's that Rolls Royce doing down there in the yard?"

"If you don't know then why did you come round here saying you want part of it?"

"Mum said something about you having a Rolls. I didn't believe a word of it."

"Okay Beryl," I said, "I think it's about time you learned what your brothers have been up to."

She looked warily at me. I continued, "And unfortunately that means we have to get on to what you've been up to."

"What are you talking about?"

"Been taking your antibiotics?"

The colour drained from her face. "What do you mean?"

"Oh, come on Beryl," I said. "You got a dose and you passed it onto me."

She looked even angrier, "Bloody Raymonde," she muttered under her breath.

"Raymonde!" I said with disbelief. "But he's queer!"

"Let's not go into that, suffice to say it was a mistake," she shuddered.

"I'm beyond caring where it came from but your bloody brothers got wind of it and assumed it was the other way round."

"So what?"

I started opening my shirt. At least she had the good grace to look shocked at the bandages. "So first off, dear Alf thought my ribs should be re-arranged, and then did much the same to the panels on the Rolls."

"Where the hell did the Rolls come into it?"

"I'd gone home to surprise you with that and ended up being evicted from my own house."

"So how did you suddenly afford that?"

"On the strength of the City contract I picked up. A job that Alf and Arthur have done their best to sabotage."

"You're just being paranoid, they wouldn't do that," she said, but she did look doubtful.

"They frightened Davidson into freezing the firm's bank account."

"Are you sure?"

"Totally bloody certain, the bank told me. The cheque I gave you bounced didn't it?"

"Well that doesn't mean it had anything to do with Alf and

Arthur," she countered.

"Okay, but having the misfortune to run into Arthur at Bullion Deposit and have him mug me of nineteen grand had something to do with them."

"What was he doing at Bullion Deposit?" she asked.

"Mugging me. For your benefit, so he said, but it looked like he was casing the place."

"How the fuck did he know you were there?"

"He didn't. It was an unfortunate coincidence."

"I really think you should stand up to them, they'd respect you more if you did."

I thought for a second how much more damaged I could get if I did that but it didn't bear thinking about.

"So let's get this straight. You had no idea I had the Roller, no idea I'd been beaten up and evicted by Alf, no idea they'd frozen the bank account, no idea I'd been mugged by Arthur? Who, by the way, said he was passing on the nineteen grand to you. And all this while I'm trying to do the contract for the Queen's visit."

"I want to be there," she said immediately. "I deserve to be there."

"Hang on, that's not the point. Are you really trying to tell me you knew nothing about any of this?"

She looked at me, slightly confused, "No," she said, then added, "Well Mum said about the car. I thought you'd scarpered with some bint."

She had no idea how near the mark that was. I thought it was best to steer away from that path.

"So your sweet siblings didn't give you a large slice of

wedge?"

"No, and I'm thinking I should be having a little word with them."

"Damned right you should, especially as it's my money."

The Dragon was desperate to go in the Roller so I told her to wait in the office while I went for a slash. I found Trish and explained what I wanted. She gave me an odd look but went off downstairs. I darted back to my office and collected the Dragon, then stopped to check that Maureen knew to do the wages.

A couple of minutes later we left the office. As we walked down, the Roller started and swung around the yard, stopping at the bottom of the stairs. Trish got out and opened the back door for the Dragon, "Good afternoon Mrs Healey," she said to Beryl, whose eyes were out on stalks. She got in and Trish closed the door and walked round to the other door with me.

"Dangerous game George," she muttered. "Dangerous game." But she smiled and opened the door for me.

I got in, the door closed gently and the Dragon immediately spat, "Who the hell is that?"

"My driver, Trish," I said as if everyone had one.

"But it's a woman," she hissed, as Trish opened her own door.

"Well I'm an equal-opportunity employer," I said smugly.

"We'll see about that," she said.

Trish turned around, "Where to Mr Healey?"

"I think we should just take a tour around the area for a

while, see if you can avoid any traffic jams," I said. "We'll need to come back here for Mrs Healey's car."

"How long should I aim for?" she replied.

"Half an hour should do it," I replied.

"An hour," the Dragon chipped in quickly.

So we drove around various roads, took in a bit of motorway, some country lanes, but the Dragon came alive as we went through towns. She sat bolt upright looking for all the world like the Queen herself, her chin up, looking down her nose at the passers-by. It's a bloody wonder she didn't start doing the royal wave.

I don't think it had been that quiet in her company ever. Happy as Larry, she was. I was careful not to catch Trish's eye in the rear view mirror. I thought how I felt about the Dragon and Trish. I have to say that even with the Dragon's blissful state, I only cared about Trish.

I thought back to the second time in the back of the Jag. That's what a man needs, I thought, someone who knows what they're doing. Unfinished business as well, I thought. I have a nasty feeling I was looking as happy as the Dragon there in the back of the Roller.

We got back to the warehouse after about an hour. The Dragon had to go back to see to the salon, something about planning the move with Raymonde. I thought she'd already done that. As she got out of the car she said, "Thank you Patricia, very smooth, very good," and scrutinised Trish's face. Then she looked at me and then back to Trish. You could hear the cogs grinding round.

"George, I'll see you back at the house later. I want to discuss these accusations of yours before I talk to my brothers."

Now, the last place I fancied being that night was back at the house with her but at least it would give me a chance to pack some more clothes.

"Right ho Beryl," I said with as much enthusiasm as I could muster.

I gave her a wave as she drove off, just a small one, careful not to jump up and down waving both arms in the air. She didn't respond.

"By Christ Trish, that woman's a hard road."

Trish came to my side, "What now then?" she said.

"We'd better get moving. Double-check the work at Mc-Cains first then the Monarch then home but keep your eye open for somewhere I can get some luggage."

"Are you going to check out of the Monarch?" she asked.

"No bloody way. I'm going to check out of home as soon as I practically can."

I sat in the front as Trish drove to McCains. "That was a bit weird," I said. "Her calling you Patricia."

"It's a power thing, calling people a name they're not known by," she said. "It is my name, so I can hardly complain, not that anyone's used it since I was a kid."

"I suppose that must be why Freeman calls me Healey to my face," I thought out loud.

"No," she said. "I reckon that's a private school thing. They go through school being called only by their surname. The only thing more friendly is when they get called some bloody nickname like stinker or fatso.

"You should be grateful that Freeman hasn't come up with

a name like carpet-tack or Axminster to taunt you with," she continued.

"They live in a funny old world, don't they?"

"To all appearances it's a tradition of honour and my-word-is-my-bond, but they're all sharks, cruising around looking for weaker creatures to eat."

"Blimey," I said. "You're not some sort of socialist are you?"

"When you've had some shark bites you get a bit wary around them."

"Doesn't put you off swimming entirely?"

"No, at that point you might as well go and work in the library."

She retreated into her own thoughts and I found myself thinking of her in a pair of glasses leaning provocatively over a pile of overdue books. I was setting off on the fantasy when I sensed the car pulling over.

"Here you are George," she said. "Luggage shop. Still open but only just by the looks of it."

There was a bloke unhooking cases from a high display outside.

"Business must be good, it's a bit early to be closing," I said. "Can you wait here?"

I went in and tried to work out what I wanted. Cases covered every surface of the interior.

"Can I help you Sir, I'm just closing but if you're quick..."

"Bit bleeding early to be closing, isn't it?"

"I have to, there's no one else to collect my little girl from school." He looked sad. "As a result, I will have to hurry you Sir."

"So you always close at three?"

"Until I get things sorted out. My missus just left me and the girl."

"Well I need a couple of decent-sized cases."

"Forgive me," he said. "But I noticed your lovely car, absolute total quality. You wouldn't want to be putting rubbish luggage in there would you?"

"So what do you suggest?"

"Well, Samsonite are the finest I have. Robust and stylish and I can do a smart set of three that nest when not in use. Fine, fine luggage."

"The most expensive, no doubt?"

"As you know from your vehicle Sir, you cannot put a price on quality."

Five minutes later I was loading the sleek aluminium cases into the vast boot of the Roller.

"He saw you coming," she laughed. "In more ways than one."

She swung the car out into the traffic and we were at Mc-Cains in short order.

I walked around the building and I have to say, their mad decision to change the carpets had transformed the place. It was quality plus and not a lot left to do either. There'd be no problem hitting the deadline. I gave myself a moment to think of the hundred and thirty grand I'd have in my grubby little hands the next morning. Okay, there was only sixty for me, but that would be pure profit.

I was still grinning when I rejoined Trish.

"You know," she said as I got in the car. "There's a lot of job satisfaction working for someone who's happy."

I just smiled, "To the Monarch, Trish."

It didn't take too long, even though we had to fill up again. I was amazed at how much money it was costing to keep the barge afloat.

When we got to the hotel, the manager was at the reception desk.

"Mr Healey," he said. "You probably don't remember dealing with me when you re-carpetted here last year." I strained to see his name tag.

"Oh yes, I remember, Mr Haycock isn't it?"

"Haycroft," he said. "Yes, we've been very pleased with it overall."

"That sounds like a 'but' in there..." I said.

"Well yes. No, we're delighted with the carpet but we had to pull up a bit in the office to accommodate some new equipment and didn't do very well putting it back."

"Okay, I'll get Keith to drop by tomorrow morning. He'll put it right in a jiff."

"That's very good of you Mr Healey," he beamed. "Any time, just ask whoever's on the desk and they can show you. Now perhaps I can get you some afternoon tea in the lounge?"

"That sounds most satisfactory," I replied. Then to Trish, "How often do we get an offer of afternoon tea?"

She smiled at Haycroft, "Very nice, thank you." He looked delighted.

As we sat with our tea in the lounge, I asked her what she wanted from life.

"If I tell you, you won't laugh?"

"Why should I?"

"Well, I've always wanted to have my own business."

"Doing what?"

"A detective agency."

"Well that's a turn-up for the books," I smiled. "Where does that come from?"

"I don't know, I seem to be able to draw people out when I talk to them and I'm good at seeing what's going on in situations. I enjoy puzzles."

For some reason, her mentioning puzzles made me think of a puzzle of my own. How was I going to get my cases packed and out of the house without the Dragon making a song and dance about it?"

"Look, I'm sorry to break this up but I need to get on the case, or cases, and phone Keith as well."

I went to the phone in reception and rang the warehouse. Keith was there, so I told him to be at the Monarch at around ten the following morning with the van and tools. He said that Maureen had managed to get everyone's wages to them and that the Jag was ready to pick up.

We drove to my house, the Dragon's house, and thankfully, her BMW was nowhere to be seen. I took a case inside and put some clothes in. I went to the study and grabbed my personal folder. Then I looked around the rest of the house and realised there wasn't really anything else I wanted. I didn't like the ornaments that she filled the place with, I didn't need anything when I came to think of it.

I took the case out and put it in the boot. I told Trish to

take herself off with the car.

"You probably want to go home but you're welcome to use the room at the hotel. It's paid for after all."

"I'll probably go back to mine," she said. "I'll get a few things and then stay at the hotel, it's handier for here in the morning. What time?"

"I want to be at McCain's at nine on the dot so I suppose around seven-thirty," I said.

"Remember it's Saturday so the traffic will be much easier," she said. "Eight should be early enough."

She drove off and I wandered round the house for a bit, found some crisps in the kitchen cupboard then sat down with a drink and turned the telly on, waiting for the Dragon to appear. The usual images of protests and politics flickered across the screen as I thought about the reality of leaving her.

Alf had so nearly brought it about but she hadn't signed up to his plan. If I was going to get away it had to be her doing the pushing. If I left of my own accord, no doubt Alf and Arthur would be beating me up until I returned.

It was all down to money really. No doubt if I had none she would boot me out in short order. Trouble was, I didn't want to be broke. There's no fun in being broke. Mind you, I wasn't having a barrel of laughs with Beryl.

I thought about the luggage guy, closing his shop early for his daughter. I didn't have anyone I would close my business early for but for Trish, I'd close the whole damned thing in a heartbeat.

When Beryl turned up she was in a strop. "Why are you dropping crisps all over the couch" she opened.

"Hello Beryl," I said. "How are the salon plans going?"

"I mean it George, why are you always making a mess?"

"It's not a mess. It's a few crumbs. I thought we were going to discuss your brothers."

"Yes, well what is there to say?" she said defensively. "They've been a bit silly and need putting straight."

"What you call silly has nearly bankrupted me and caused me a great deal of physical distress," I said angrily. "When are you going to admit they're a bloody menace to everyone around them?"

"Look George, they might be a bit boisterous but I have to be sure of my facts if I'm going to confront them. You're probably putting it on for effect, milking it for some sympathy?"

"As God is my witness Beryl, it's all just as I said."

"So if you were all innocent in this, why did you run?"

Ah, time for some elaboration.

"To be honest Beryl, Alf put such a scare into me, I thought it would be wise to lay low for a bit."

"So where have you been laying low?" she looked suspiciously at me.

"I checked in to a hotel."

"What hotel?"

"The Monarch."

"Oh I see. All right for some," she said.

"It's just a hotel Beryl, I happen to have done some carpet there last year."

"I hope you got a discount then," she snapped.

As things slipped back into our usual way of carrying on, I was tempted to just walk away. When it came down to it, I was only hanging around for the nine grand balance I hadn't promised Beryl for her salon out of the cash Arthur had taken off me. But then again, it would be good to see the bastards put right by their sister.

"Strikes me Beryl, that you don't really want to put them right because you'd have to let on what you were up to."

"That wouldn't have happened if you'd been more of a man," she spat.

"That's ridiculous, a man like Raymonde?"

"Raymonde understands women," she said.

"Come off it," I said. "Of course he understands women, he's a gay hairdresser!"

"He's bi actually," she said.

"He's what?"

"Bi, bi-sexual, it means he swings both ways."

"You mean he's a sex maniac?"

"I'm drawing a line under what happened, it would be a good idea if you did too, if you want to get this money back. We just need to work out the right way to get the result we want."

The 'we' struck me a bit odd, were we a team all of a sudden?

"So what do you propose?"

"It would be a good idea to meet them on neutral ground. Somewhere in public, how about the Monarch?"

I thought somehow that this was a really bad idea but I couldn't see why. I couldn't think of an alternative that made any sense either.

"Okay," I said, "I've got to go down to the City first thing. Can we meet there around eleven?"

"I'll see if I can persuade them."

"It might be an idea to keep it as just a meeting between you and them, no mention of me." I was thinking how I seemed to get the brothers a bit over-excited.

"I'll get on the phone," she said as she left the room.

In the morning, I woke early. I was eager to get down to McCain's but there was nothing I could do but wait till eight. I drank some coffee and then drank some more. I even looked through the kitchen and found some cereal to eat. I started thinking about what to do with sixty-six grand. Where to go seemed like a more relevant question. I had no particular dreams of going to wild, exotic foreign parts. I had no ties to anywhere except around where I had spent my entire life.

It struck me that I would probably be happiest in the area where all this shit had happened. I wondered why that would be when it was nothing but grief. Perhaps I had no imagination.

On the dot of eight the Roller pulled up at the entrance to the drive. I shook myself out of the odd mood I was in and almost bounded out to the car. I knew the Dragon would be watching so I kept cool and walked slowly. Clever Trish opened the back door for me.

"Good girl," I said. "Good morning."

"Good morning George, I mean Mr Healey."

We drove away and I caught a glimpse of the Dragon looking out from her room. Trish pointed the Spirit of Ecstasy towards the City. There was no traffic and we arrived early.

I asked Trish to wait. It certainly made parking less of a hassle having a driver.

I looked up at the grand entrance to the McCain Sullivan building. Impressive, solid, dependable.

I went in and asked for Mr Freeman. I stood in the lobby for about twenty minutes with the jobsworth behind the desk giving me filthy looks. Eventually the lift opened and Pevsner came out carrying a file. I shuddered.

"Hello Mr Healey," he said, polishing his glasses. "What can we do for you?"

"I've come for the balance of the money for the carpet contract. It was finished last night, on schedule."

"Yes, it was in a way, but there's a problem."

"What's that?" I asked. "Is it not finished?"

"Yes, it's finished but it's not the right colour."

"It's dark blue."

"But not Royal Blue."

"That's splitting hairs," I protested. "It's what everyone would understand to be Royal Blue."

"But not Royal Blue," he said, then opened the file. "It says here in the contract which you signed that the colour of the carpet would be Royal Blue. I'm afraid that you are in breach of contract and consequently we owe you nothing."

"Leave it out. You can't do that. You needed a carpet in a hurry and I supplied it, now pony up."

"Mr Healey," he said nastily. "You're small fry. If you want to swim with the big fishes, make sure you've got teeth. We will not be paying a penny more. And by the way, you can rest assured that even if you had supplied Royal Blue, we would have found some other way of not paying you."

"You can't do this, you bastard!"

"I'm employed to do this, and I'm good at it," he said smugly. "You should have asked for more than twenty percent up front."

"I'll sue you!" I shouted.

"Go ahead," he said quietly. "But make sure you have deep pockets. Lawyers are not cheap."

"You bastards!" was the best I could come up with as I was escorted from the building.

I looked up and down the street, caught sight of the car and headed towards it. I felt sick and unsteady. As I reached it Trish jumped out and said, "Are you okay George? You look awful. Is something wrong?"

I couldn't answer. I just got into the car and sat there hurting all over. I was staring without seeing anything, my head was throbbing, stomach churning. I opened the door, leant out over the road and was sick. Trish sat behind the wheel, wide-eyed with confusion.

"What ever is the matter George? Did someone hit you?" she said.

"In a manner of speaking, yes," I managed to gasp. "And I

thought my relatives were bad."

"What do you want me to do?" she asked.

"Well there's no point hanging around here, we may as well head for the hotel."

$\mathbf{M}$y mind span all the way back. I kept grasping parts of the implications of what had happened, only to have them replaced by others. I managed to explain what had gone on to Trish and she was good enough not to say 'I told you'.

In the background of my thoughts was the suspicion it was a bad dream but it seemed real enough. I couldn't really say my life's work had disappeared but you don't get breaks like that very often. So much for the big decision of how or where to spend the money, I thought.

If there was no way I could fight those thieving bastards, I would have to find some other way of paying the fitters their other half and Eddie for his bloody Midnight Blue. What had seemed like a trivial amount to take out of a hundred and thirty grand now looked like a bloody mountain to climb. I'd be doing poxy deals for the rest of my working. The Roller would have to go, the Jag probably too. I'd have to find some way of persuading the Dragon to curb her ambitions for the salon. And unless I got her on side, I'd be homeless. Shit, shit, shit, I thought.

My head was still spinning when we got back to the Monarch. The whole feeling of driving up to the grand house felt all wrong. The perfect paintwork, the neat fences, the smooth gravel, the flower beds being tended by a gardener, the smart cars parked away from the house all suddenly seemed to mock me. I felt like it wasn't my place to be there any longer.

What looked totally wrong though was seeing Keith's scruffy transit parked outside. No doubt even Tim the bell boy was repelled by the toxic nature of it. It took me a sec to remember that I knew he would be there and it brought me back to the present. I got Trish to drop me and while she parked, I went to see how Keith was doing. As I walked into reception, the girl said, "Oh Mr Healey, your fitter is here."

"Yes," I said. "I noticed," nodding at the van outside.

"He's certainly getting on with it. We were just organising a cup of tea for him, would you like one too?"

"Yes, that would be great," I replied. "Perhaps one for Trish too?"

"For Mrs Healey? Certainly."

Hello, I thought, that might be a tad awkward when the real Mrs Healey turned up.

She picked up the phone and spoke to whoever was making tea. I mimed going through to the office and she stood aside to let me pass just as Trish was coming in to the hotel. I saw where Keith was beavering away and I heard the receptionist say "Ah, Mrs Healey, your husband has just gone through to the office. If you wait here, we're just rustling up a cup of tea."

Keith was nearly finished when the tea arrived.

"What's up Guv?" he said as he slurped his drink. "You don't look full of the joys."

"Those fuckers at McCains have stitched us up."

"You mean they didn't have the money ready?"

"No, Keith," I said wearily. "They didn't, and they're not

going to, ever. They're refusing to pay and that sharp little shit Pevsner has got it all worked out legally. I'm fucked."

"That's a blow Guv," he said. "What can you do?"

"I suppose we'll just have to keep doing what we do," I said, resigned. "Laying carpet."

"What about the fitters?" he asked.

"They're just going to have to wait, along with Eddie."

"What about my bonus?" he asked.

"When I said I was fucked, I should have said we're all fucked." I said. "Now let's get this place tidied up."

He went around the room picking up scraps he'd cut off, bits of gripper and his tools. As he left, I noticed a piece of gripper he'd missed and picked it up. He set off for the van and I followed.

As we walked out towards the van, my heart sank as I saw Arthur and Alf walking towards the hotel, and us. A second or two later they saw us just as the Dragon's BMW came up the drive. Alf came straight towards me shouting: "George Fucking Healey, I told you to stay away from our family!" He came steaming towards me drawing his fist back as he came closer.

I'd had enough.

"Fuck off Alf," I said, and lashed out at his head with the gripper strip. Suddenly he stopped in his tracks with a curtain of blood flowing down his face from the cut it had made across his forehead.

"Fuck, he's blinded me, get him Arthur," he shouted. Arthur accelerated to get past Keith, who swung his knee kicker and caught Arthur on the side of the head. He went down like a ninepin, spark out.

"Bloody Hell," I said.

"Bloody Hell," said Keith.

The Dragon jumped out of her car. "What the bloody hell do you think you're doing?" she shouted. I looked towards her and realised she was shouting at her brothers. I almost laughed.

Alf was spinning around unsteadily, unable to see through the blood, trying to work out where the Dragon's shouts were coming from. Arthur was groaning on the floor. Beryl marched over to the gardener who was standing with his mouth wide open and relieved him of the hose, which she first turned on Alf's face and then at Arthur's head.

"You stupid bloody fuckers," she shouted at them. "When I need you to interfere in my business I will ask you. How dare you take it upon yourselves to be my bloody minders."

I was standing with my mouth open and I wasn't the only one. Keith and Alf were also looking amazed. Arthur was sitting on the deck shaking his head slowly like an old dog. I looked towards the hotel and caught sight of Trish through the window laughing herself silly.

Time had slowed up while all this was happening but then started approaching normal speed again.

"I came here for a meeting," said the Dragon. "So let's go in and have a meeting, if they'll let us in after all this nonsense. Keith, we don't need you, so pack your van and hop it." Keith looked relieved.

I was keeping a wary eye on Alf as I gave Keith the blood-stained gripper but to my amazement Alf appeared to be keeping a wary eye on me as he dabbed at his forehead with a handkerchief. Arthur slowly got to his feet blinking hard. We made our way slowly inside as Keith's van pulled away.

The receptionist just nodded as we passed by, Trish was sitting on the window seat like butter wouldn't melt.

The Dragon said, "We're having a meeting in the lounge, get some tea sent in if you please."

"Alf," the Dragon continued. "Go and get yourself cleaned up, then come straight back here, you've got some explaining to do. Arthur, sit there, George, you sit there."

Arthur still looked groggy but did as he was told. I was happy to sit where she said.

The receptionist brought in a tray of tea things and set them down on the table between Arthur and me. The Dragon sat down next to me.

After a minute Alf came back in, glanced around the table and sat next to his brother. They sat there scowling at their sister. Barely a glance for me.

"Right," she said. "Arthur, where's this nineteen grand you took from George for me?"

Arthur groaned again. "I hadn't got around to getting it to you," he said guiltily.

"And how long was that going to take, may I ask?"

Arthur looked down at his tea cup.

"Alf," Alf looked up from the table at her. "When you eavesdrop other people's conversations, make sure you've got the right end of the stick."

I was beginning to enjoy this despite the morning's events.

"And when you feel the need to protect my reputation, you

bloody well wait till you are asked."

"George," she turned to me. "What's happening to my front-row ticket for the Queen's visit?" I knew it couldn't last, but at mention of Her Majesty my brothers-in-law suddenly perked up.

"They've fucked me over," I said, "I'm not even getting paid let alone getting to see the Queen."

"Why not?" she asked.

"They waited till the job was finished and then got the lawyers to wriggle out of paying."

"So how much are you in the hole?" How did she even know such terms?

"A hundred and thirty-three grand," I admitted.

"It seems to me that your money and the royal visit can be connected."

"Of course they're connected," I protested. "They wanted the new carpet for the Queen's visit."

"You're not following," she said. "The key to both locks must be in the hands of the same person. Who's the boss?"

I noticed that the brothers were showing much more interest now.

"Franklin B Sullivan, CEO of McCain Sullivan, American. He seems to get his thrills ripping off bits of Olde England."

"How do you mean?"

"First thing he boasted about was destroying Colesham Hall and lifting the library panelling and fireplace for his office."

Arthur blinked several times and then said, "Colesham Hall, I know Colesham Hall, they demolished it."

"That much we gather Arthur," the Dragon addressed him like a slow child. "What of it?"

"They built a flash new place on the site," he said, but looked puzzled. "What's this about Her Majesty?"

"George has fitted a new carpet in a building the Queen is visiting on Monday," she said. "Keep up Arthur."

He frowned, "I want to see Her Majesty."

She nodded, "You're not the only one. Now how do we get hold of Franklin B Sullivan?"

I thought of how Trish had shown me up the day before. "We could look in the phone book," I suggested.

I went out to reception to find a phone book. Trish was still there.

"How's it going?" she asked.

"We need to track down Franklin B-loody Sullivan at home," I replied. I got the phone book from the receptionist and started looking through it for Sullivans. There were a bunch of them but no Fs, FBs or Franklins.

"Damn," I said. "No joy."

"Does he live in this area?" Trish asked.

"All we know is that he demolished Colesham Hall and might have built a new house on the site."

Trish's eyes lit up. "Can I use the car for an hour?"

"Where do you need to go?" I asked.

"I'll start with the library, it's a shame Companies House isn't open at the weekend."

"Go to it girl, but if you find anything, ring back here and tell me."

I went back in to the lounge.

"No joy in the phone book but Trish has gone to the library to do some digging," I said.

"Who the hell is Trish?" said Alf.

"George's driver," said the Dragon, looking pained.

Arthur roused himself, "Why don't we just go to where Colesham Hall was and start kicking over stones?"

"How far away is it?" asked Alf.

"Only about thirty minutes."

"Let's go then," Alf started to get up.

"Wait, wait, wait," the Dragon said. "Even if he is there and you get to speak to him, what are you going to do?"

"Persuade him to let us meet Her Majesty," Alf said with a nasty smile.

"And if he says yes, how do you know you won't be arrested when you try to get near the Queen? And what about the hundred and thirty grand he's weaselled out of paying?"

"We'll just have to persuade him a lot," Alf retorted.

"You really are a couple of planks," she said. "We need to make a plan, make a backup plan. Think with our brains not our fists."

"I suppose we could make a couple of calls to see if anyone knows anyone who knows," Alf said.

"Now you're thinking straight, get on with it," said Beryl.

Alf and Arthur went out to use the phone in reception leaving the Dragon and me.

"I didn't know you had it in you," she said, pouring herself another cup and looking admiringly at me. It was unnerving.

"Neither did I," I said. "You seem to have put them straight though."

After about half an hour, the receptionist came in and said I had a call. I went out and picked up the phone on the desk.

"Hello, George Healey here," I said.

It was Trish.

"I've been going through newspapers and directories," she

said. "Colesham Hall was redeveloped and sold on. Some-body called Tims lives there now."

"Damn," I said. "A dead end then?"

"Well, actually, there's been some interesting things about McCain Sullivan in the business pages."

"What's that then?"

"They seem to sail very close to the wind. Nothing they can be copped for, but there seem to be lots of rumours."

"Perhaps the Queen's visit is to make them kosher?"

"Perhaps. Anyhow, there was a profile of Franklin B and it mentioned him living in a mansion in Mill Hill. I've checked the phone books but he must be ex-directory. That's the best I can do for now."

"That's great," I said. "Come on back to the hotel."

I replaced the phone and found the boys.

"Got any contacts in Mill Hill?" I asked.

"People who know people, I'm sure," Alf said and went into a huddle with Arthur. It looked dangerous to me but then they broke apart and Alf said, "See if they know other cab companies nearer to Mill Hill."

Arthur nodded his agreement and went back to the phone. Alf turned to me, the slash across his forehead blood-raw and bruised, "George, you seem to have invented a new weapon. Well done."

I didn't know what to say so I just tried to do a hard smile, it probably came out all wrong.

The Dragon came out of the lounge, "Any progress?" she asked.

"We've discovered he's not at Colesham Hall but somewhere in Mill Hill. Your brothers are tracking cab companies."

"Good," she said. "Someone's using their brains."

The girl on reception asked if we could go back to the lounge as we were making it difficult for other guests to get through. Alf gave a look but complied. The Dragon and I followed leaving Arthur, who was still on the phone.

I waited a few minutes then made as if to go for a slash. As I went through reception I checked that Arthur was busy talking and then leaned over the desk to the receptionist.

"Claire," I said, reading her name tag. "Please don't get my driver Trish confused with Mrs Healey," ducking my head towards the lounge.

She looked baffled for a sec then looked between me and the lounge, "Certainly, Mr Healey, not a problem."

To say I was relieved was understating it. I could do without misunderstandings in that company.

Arthur came off the phone. "Looks like we've got a result," he said, walking with me back to the lounge.

"I've got hold of a limo company in Barnet who have a certain McCain Sullivan as account holders. They often pick up Sullivan and his missus to go up West for the theatre or opera."

"So we have the address?" said Alf.

"Better," said Arthur.

"What do you mean?"

Arthur smiled triumphantly. "They've booked a limo this evening to go to Covent Garden, pick up from their house."

The Dragon looked at me. "Your Trish can pick them up in the Roller," she said.

171

'Your' Trish? I thought.

"Hang on," said Arthur. "There's something else. They always have a bodyguard with them."

"Is that a problem?" I asked.

Arthur gave me a withering look and got back on the phone, organising the car substitution.

It was like the wagon train as we pulled out of the Monarch, Trish in the Rolls, Alf and Arthur in their respective Jag and Rover, the Dragon and me in her BMW all heading for Mill Hill. Arthur peeled off to collect some gear and a couple of mates, having arranged that we all meet at The Good Earth.

Now personally, I'm not so enamoured of Chinese food, especially at lunchtime, but the point was everyone knew where it was. When we got there it was closed so we just parked up and waited for everyone to arrive. When we were all gathered, we huddled in and around Beryl's BMW and sorted out who was going to do what.

I was in with Arthur and his mates, who Arthur introduced as Nobby and Pete. Pete nodded at me and grunted, Nobby said nothing. The road leading past Sullivan's house was narrow like a country lane even though we were just a couple of miles from civilisation. We were parked a couple of hundred yards away from The Cedars in a little passing place but could just see the entrance gates. Alf and the Dragon were ready to do their bit, parked a couple of hundred yards beyond the house. They were in Beryl's BMW. Alf and Arthur had used Alf's Jag to suss the place earlier and had left it at

The Good Earth.

The limo had been booked for six and at five-to Trish came past us in the Roller. She stopped at the gates of The Cedars and after a wait of a minute at the gates, drove in.

I was shitting myself as we waited for the thing to unfold. Arthur and Nobby seemed cool as cucumbers. Five minutes later, the Rolls emerged from the gates and turned towards the Dragon's BMW, where hopefully they had set up a fake puncture for her, leaving not enough space to get past. The idea was that Trish would stop, Alf would disable the body guard and accompany the Sullivans as they followed Beryl to the junction half-a-mile ahead, turning around and returning to the house.

We waited. I handed ciggies around and we all lit up. Sometimes I love a cig, enjoy every drag but other times I can't wait to finish them. I was nervously pulling big drags, trying to speed up time. It didn't help. I opened the window to toss the butt end and headlights approached the house from the other direction.

Arthur started the Rover and pulled forward. We got to the gates as the other cars were going in and joined the queue. We pulled up in a line on the carriage driveway, Rolls first, outside the front door. Arthur and Nobby piled out and I saw that Arthur had a gun in his hand and Nobby a little bag. I figured I would wait a minute or two before joining them. I didn't really want to be anywhere near guns.

Nobby scanned the outside of the house, went to the Roller and had a quick conversation, reached in and then turned towards the front door with the keys in his hand. While he was fiddling with the door I was looking at the other cars but couldn't see any bodyguard. Perhaps they'd been mistaken about that, I thought. Nobby went inside and after a few minutes reappeared giving an all-clear signal.

I watched as Alf and Arthur escorted the Sullivans from the Rolls towards the house. They weren't waving their guns around but had them in their hands. Pete tagged along. Franklin's missus looked petrified but Franklin himself was scowling and looking around like he wanted to remember who was there and what they looked like. They went in and the Dragon followed. She turned at the door and signalled for Me and Trish to follow.

I went over to Trish.

"Did that go okay?" I asked her.

"I suppose so," she said a bit shakily. "Your brother-in-law is not a nice man." She looked a bit shell-shocked to be honest.

"Why? What happened?" I said.

She shook her head and shuddered, "I'll tell you about it later."

We headed into the house. There were paintings on the walls of the hallway. Some looked like big versions of greetings cards, others like kid's pictures. Nobby was busying himself with his bag of tricks. I could hear Franklin B kicking off through an open door on our left.

"I don't know what the hell you're after but you can be damned sure I'll catch up with you. You're not even smart enough to hide your faces."

175

"Shut up" came Alf's dulcet growl.

"Everything's alarmed, you can't touch anything without setting them off, the police will get here in minutes."

"If you don't shut your trap, I'll shut it for you," Alf said quietly. "In a minute, your alarms will be fucked, so let's calm down eh?"

There was a pause before Nobby wandered into the room ahead of us.

"Okay guv, the alarms are no trouble any more."

Me and Trish walked in. Franklin B did a double-take. "Healey! What the hell are you doing here?"

I looked around the room. Right bloody posh it was. Fancy fireplace, fancy wallpaper, fancy curtains and more paintings all around. It made me sick, all that wealth, probably nicked off the less fortunate. Pete was looking all round the room but in a different way. He was feeling along the edges of pictures, along skirtings, testing carpet to see if it was loose. He went off to explore other rooms.

"You know what I'm doing here," I replied. "You owe me a hundred and thirty-three thousand pounds for honest work well done. It doesn't look like you can't afford it."

"Now that's just a misunderstanding," he protested. "You'll be getting your money."

"Damned right I will but your lawyer rat Mr Pevsner made it very plain you wouldn't be paying. So where does that leave us?"

"Hey, c'mon," he said. "Those guys are just a bit keen, wanting to impress me."

"You and I both know that's shit. I was happy to have my

bill paid but now it's gone up by fifty percent," I said. "So by my reckoning and rounding things up to the nearest whole number that makes two hundred grand."

"You're mad," he said. "I don't keep that sort of money lying around here."

"I'll take cash or bank draft."

"No, really, I don't have anything here."

"Prove it," I said. "Show me your safe."

"I don't have a safe."

Pete piped up, "There's two safes. One's obvious, behind a picture in the study, the other's a bit clever." The blood drained out of Sullivan's face.

"Where's that then?" said Alf.

"Behind floor to ceiling book shelves in the library," he sounded delighted. "It's a quality piece of work. Very tasty."

"You don't need to look in the safes," said Franklin B. "These pictures are worth at least two hundred grand, each."

Alf, Arthur, Pete, Nobby, the Dragon and me all looked round the room and shook our heads.

Trish said, "Impressionists, very valuable at auction at the moment."

"How the fuck do you know that?" I asked her.

"It pays to know what turns your customers on," she said.

I looked from her to Sullivan and back again in disbelief.

"No, not Franklin B here," she smiled. "He's not the only one who loves an impressionist."

"She's right," said Franklin. "Take a picture, take two, hell, take three. I'll not report them stolen, I'll give you receipts here and now so you can do whatever you like with them."

177

"He's got a point," Trish said. "You'd actually be better off long-term."

At this point Alf chipped in, "It's all very well you paying George's bill with these pictures, but what about us meeting Her Majesty?"

"I can't do that," he spluttered. "You'd need clearance from Special Branch."

Alf smiled, "Oh they know me, and I know them. That shouldn't be a problem. You just need to call them and tell them you want us there, I'll do the rest."

Sullivan looked panicky, "But what if we don't want you there? You'll be out of place."

"You mean because we're villains or because we don't know an impressionist from a play school painting?" Alf asked mildly.

"Hang on," I said to Sullivan. "Are you sure you've got no cash here?"

"What's wrong with the paintings?" he said. "You're much better off with them."

"Yeah, you've said. But cash is king really, isn't it?"

"There is no cash to speak of, maybe a few thousand. I don't keep cash, I'm not a bank."

"Okay, let's sort out the receipts," I said. "Which ones should I take, Trish?"

Trish looked around the room and picked out a blue one, an orange one and a greeny-grey one.

"How do we know these are kosher?" I asked Sullivan.

"I've got the provenances in my safe," he said.

"What's that?"

"All the paperwork that shows the painting's history and ownership."

"Well it seems to me that you and me should go into your study and do a little paperwork. Could you join us Alf?"

Alf grunted and waved his gun vaguely at Sullivan.

Franklin B got up slowly and moved to a doorway at the far end of the enormous room.

The study was somewhat smaller but still bigger than our lounge and our lounge wasn't small. Sullivan went to a picture of a foggy sea and pulled it, frame and all, like a door. He fiddled with the dial that was revealed and after some toing and froing the safe door opened. Alf moved in close with his gun held up.

"Just let me have a little look first," he said.

Alf shoved his hand into the opening and patted around in both shelves. He came out with a pile of notes, probably not more than five grand even if they were fifties. He slipped them into his jacket pocket and waved his gun at Sullivan to continue with the safe contents. Franklin B pulled out a big pile of folders and put them on the desk then sorted through them, taking three out and returning the rest to the safe.

He handed them to me. "That's the provenances. Now I'll write you some receipts." He got some headed paper and a pen and started writing.

"Who shall I make them out to?" he asked.

"Just leave a blank and we can fill it in later," growled Alf.

"Okay. I'll have to put how much you have paid me for them too."

"Why don't we just say sixty-six thousand for each?" I said.

He continued writing up the paperwork. As I watched, I wondered why he was being so cooperative. He obviously loved the paintings and wouldn't let them go easily unless he had some trick up his sleeve to get them back. He could go to the rozzers and complain that they'd been stolen, but we'd have the receipts to show that they weren't. There had to be another angle.

I thought back to his reaction when Pete had said there were two safes. That was what had made him suddenly give up his precious paintings. There had to be something worth more in the second safe. He'd finished writing, so I gathered the folders and the receipts together.

"Hold on," he said. "Can I just take copies for my records?"

I shrugged my shoulders and handed back the receipts. He went to a copy machine in the corner and fed them in. It must have been one of those deluxe ones because the copies came out instantly. He handed the originals back to me.

"Alf," I said. "I think it would be remiss of us not to check the second safe. After all, there might be enough cash in there to make all this paintings shit seem like too much grief."

Sullivan looked terrified. It was an amazing reaction, he broke out in a sweat.

"I tell you, there's nothing in the other safe," he said.

"Nothing?" I said. "Then why don't we just have a little look to check?"

"There's just some company paperwork. Legal stuff, nothing."

Alf leaned towards him. "Now why don't you just set our minds at rest by showing us?"

He looked from Alf to me and back again. Alf continued, "Or Pete will just blow the door off. He's very good, been doing it man and boy for years."

Sullivan's shoulders sagged and he nodded, resigned.

We went into the library and I have to say it was some classy room. Books from floor to ceiling with built in ladders that slid sideways so you could get at any books. It was like a magic trick when Sullivan aligned a ladder with a particular shelf, touched what looked like a regular part of the books and a whole section opened up revealing another numbered dial. He turned it to and fro and then grasped the big handles together and swung it open.

Again, Alf had a little feel for offensive weapons and then drew out a pile of papers which he glanced at, shrugged and handed to me. I looked at them and it seemed to be exactly as Franklin B had said. A bunch of legal papers. I didn't really understand any of it, it was all to do with shares and and share prices. Gobbledegook basically to my eyes, but I couldn't help thinking it was something valuable to him.

"Looks like you're right," I said. He suddenly relaxed. I continued, "I'll just take copies of these and then we can be out of your hair."

He made a lunge for the papers but Alf just grabbed his upper arm with his free hand and held him.

"Don't be silly now, you might get hurt," Alf muttered in his ear.

I went back to the study, did two sets of copies and then returned to the library, giving Sullivan his originals. He looked miserable and desperate.

"Now this is a bit handy," I said. "You don't seem to want these documents escaping. I'll keep these copies safe, but if I get any grief from you, they'll find a way out. Understood?"

He looked daggers at me.

"Right," said Alf. "Let's get these phone calls made for the arrangements on Monday and then we can be on our way."

Back at the house, I woke up on Sunday morning with the feeling I'd just had the weirdest nightmare. It took a while for me to realise that it hadn't been a dream. I lay there in bed thinking over the previous evening's events.

After we'd relieved Sullivan of his precious information, we had taken it with the paintings and the documentation, the proverthingies, outside to the Roller. Trish had opened the boot and I had bloody nearly had a heart attack. The Sullivans' bodyguard had been trussed up and thrown in there.

Alf, Arthur and Pete had hauled him out and over to the front steps, where they had seemed to have a little heart-to-heart with him. He had done a lot of nodding and had then sat there immobile and still gagged and bound with gaffer tape while we had gone about our business.

The paintings had been split between Alf, Arthur and the Dragon while I had held onto what I had started thinking of as the insurance policy along with the receipts. What the others hadn't seen had been me separating the two set of copies I'd made and tucking one under the carpet in the boot of the Roller.

We had gone our separate ways although unfortunately that meant Trish and me going separate ways too and here I was, back in the house with the Dragon, although she had been curiously quiet.

I rolled out of bed as fast as my ribs allowed and immediately checked that the insurance was still where I'd put it under the mattress before I'd gone to sleep. I got dressed and started reading it as I went downstairs. I have to say, it made no sense to me. There were loads of names and figures and dates and references to companies and brokers. As I say, it made no sense to me but I did want to know what it was about.

The Dragon came downstairs and announced that her mate Steph was going to be coming round to help her work out what she was going to wear to meet the Queen. I could see that the rest of the day was going to be a right-off unless I got out of there fast. I was just making plans in my mind when I remembered the fitters.

"Beryl," I said. "Before you start on all that, can we just straighten out some business?"

"I hope you're not going to ruin my day," she retorted.

"I don't know if you remember but yesterday's dramas all started when that fucker Sullivan tried to wriggle out of paying. I've still got to pay my fitters, and Eddie for the carpet. Can you get that cash of mine out of Arthur because we won't be able to sell the painting for weeks, probably months."

"Sell the painting?" she said. "Why would I sell the painting? It'll lend this house a bit of class. Mind you we'll need to redecorate to really enhance it."

"But we've got to sell the painting, that's my entire profit for the McCain job, and it's not even all profit. Eddie is down for thirty-three grand of that and I've still got to pay my fitters pretty bloody soon."

"Oh, don't be silly George," she said. "Now that you're getting on so well with Alf and Arthur, you could go and ask them yourself. They'll be down the Highwayman at lunchtime, they always are on a Sunday."

"Oh great," I said. "How the hell am I going to get there?"

"Well, don't look at me, I thought you had a driver at your disposal?"

I gave her a filthy look and went to the phone. I rang the Monarch but there was nobody in my room there. In all the excitement of the previous few days, I had neglected to get Trish's home number. I ordered a cab and stood around kicking my heels till it arrived, I was still hopeful that Trish was somewhere at the Monarch so decided to go there first. Then I started worrying about having two copies of Sullivan's secret document in the Roller so I decided to go to the warehouse first. As soon as I got in the back, the driver started droning on about how he spent his spare time treasure hunting with a metal detector. I gave it two minutes before I gave him an ultimatum: tip or chat. He soon buttoned it.

Thank Christ Keith had shown me Maureen's security system. It only took me a couple of minutes to have the filing cabinet drawer open in front of me. I stood there looking at all the folders wondering where to put it then tucked the papers into a one marked 'Insurance'. I was just locking the cabinet when I thought that might be a bit obvious, so I opened it again and moved them to 'Vat'.

At the Monarch I did a quick search of the car park to see if the Roller was there. There was no sign of it so I headed for reception. The one that wasn't the manager or Claire was on duty. I looked at her badge.

"Sarah love," I said. "Have you seen my car or my driver since yesterday?"

She looked at me for a moment, frowned, and then brightened up. "Oh yes Mr Healey," she said. "Your driver left a note for you, Trish isn't it? Hang on, I'll just get it."

She went off to the office behind and reappeared with a folded piece of paper which she handed to me.

"There you are Mr Healey, she left that yesterday evening."

I unfolded the note, there was nothing except a phone number. Well, I say nothing, but actually there was a lip print as well. I stood there staring at it. An odd warmth suddenly spread all over me and I found myself smiling. Such a simple thing yet in that instant I knew I wanted to be with Trish, how could I not?

"Are you all right Mr Healey?" Sarah sounded concerned.

"Fine, fine, can I use the phone?"

She pointed to the end of the desk. "Of course."

Then she continued, "Not that it's any of my business Mr Healey, but do you actually need your room here? You don't seem to have used it for two days."

I paused for a instant, thinking of Trish.

"Now more than ever," I said and started dialling.

The ring tone went on for ages, I prayed she'd answer. I stood there trying to look calm while my insides turned cartwheels. It must have been about the fortieth ring before she answered.

"Any chance you can do some overtime today?" I asked her.

"Who is this?" she answered. I was floored.

"It's George. George Healey, your bleeding employer," I hissed.

"All right, all right George, just mucking you about, keep your hair on," she laughed. "What's up?"

"I have to get to the Highwayman's so I need the car."

"Sure," she said. "I'll pop over to the hotel as soon as my hair's dry."

"How long will that be?"

"I should be there within an hour."

Which left me an hour to go to the room and have a leisurely bath and get into some clean clothes since Trish had offloaded my case. Not just offloaded it but hung everything up as well. I sat on the bed and thought about the document. Why had he been so keen to keep it to himself? I wasn't sure but I thought I might have heard of one or two of the names that were on it. They seemed familiar, but not people I knew so I suppose they must have been in the papers or something like that.

There was a light tap at the door and my heart jumped. I let Trish in.

"Hello George, why the frown?"

"I was trying to think why Sullivan was so keen to hide that document."

"Any ideas then?" she said.

"No, not really. You?"

"I never saw it."

"Of course," I said. "The copy is in the boot of the car. I'll go and get it."

"Well why don't we go downstairs and have a coffee?"

"Good idea. You order some while I get the document."

Ten minutes later, we sat in the lounge with coffee and the pages of the document spread over the table in front of us. Trish had glanced through several of them.

"Got any ideas?" I said.

"I'm not sure. I think it's something to do with shares. I tell you what though, I know one or two of these names."

"Where from? I thought I recognised a couple from the papers or the news."

"No George," she looked thoughtful. "I've met one or two of these."

"Where?" I asked.

"Not sure you want to know, actually."

I had to think about that for a moment or two, but then the penny dropped.

"Okay," I said. "Work contacts then?"

"You could say that, although one of them is a right bastard."

We were both quiet for a couple of minutes. Eventually Trish broke the silence.

"So why have you got to get to the Highwayman?" she said.

"I have to persuade Arthur to give up the cash he took off me so I can pay the fitters tomorrow. Still leaves me a shed-load short though."

"But you can sell the painting can't you?"

"That would take weeks, and the Dragon has taken a fancy to it. Apparently it'll lend the house a bit of fucking class"

"Well why don't we think about these names while we go to the Highwayman's and see if you can get the cash out of your new best-buddy brother-in-law?"

 W e drove mostly in silence. I was thinking mixed-up thoughts of bits of paper. One showing names I half knew and one showing a lip print. I couldn't really concentrate on either as the other kept intruding. Trish seemed to be thinking hard too but I bet it was just about the names she knew.

Eventually she broke the silence, "You know what I think?"

"That we should go to the Caribbean?" I said hopefully.

"No, about the information," she laughed.

"I have no idea. I don't understand it at all," I said.

"Okay. It's got to be something dodgy otherwise he wouldn't have been so keen to keep it secret, yes?"

"That makes sense."

"So, in his world, dodgy must mean something illegal, against City regulations, wouldn't you say?"

"Uh huh."

"So, what kind of stuff is against the rules in the City?"

"Same as anywhere else, I'd have thought, robbery, murder that sort of thing."

"And rigging the game. Like having a tip that your horse has been nobbled. If you bet on some share going up, knowing full well that it will because you have some inside info, that's not allowed."

"So why does the list of names and dates and sums add up to that?"

"I'm not sure but it could easily be something like that."

"So they obviously want to hide it?"

"I think they would pay a lot to keep it hidden," she said thoughtfully. "Perhaps three impressionists is cheap if the alternative is prison."

The Highwayman was one of those big gin palaces on Watling Street, what used to be called a road-house. A big pub with several bars, some guest rooms and a massive car park. It was well past its prime which had probably been in the fifties. No wonder my brothers-in-law were regulars.

We parked up and went in but it took a few minutes of checking out various bars before we found Alf and Arthur. They were holding court in the middle of a crowd of dodgy-looking riff-raff. Alf was sporting a heavily-scabbed forehead but didn't seem unhappy about it. He was waving a large cocktail and telling a story that he obviously thought was side-splitting. The group were dutifully splitting their sides. We went up to the bar, found ourselves some stools and ordered a couple of drinks. I waited till Alf had delivered his punchline then went over and asked Arthur for a word outside.

Arthur scowled at me, glanced at Alf, nodded and followed me out to the car park. He lit a ciggie without offering me one.

"I hope you're not thinking that because of what went on last night, we're pals or anything like that?"

"God forbid," I said. "But since Beryl's put you straight over that little misunderstanding last week, I thought you could return my cash, now that she's not going to need it."

"Cash?" he said. "I don't know anything about any cash, you're imagining things."

"The cash you took off me at the Bullion storage," I said.

"Like I'm saying George, I don't know what you're talking about and I don't appreciate the accusation."

I shook my head. Keith should have hit him a bloody site harder, I thought.

"It's not an accusation Arthur, it's a fact. You owe me nineteen thousand, four hundred and forty-four quid, in cash."

His eyes narrowed and he grabbed me by the lapels and lifted me, then slammed my back against the nearest car. The jolt sent pains all over my ribcage and made my eyes water.

"It seems like you're a bit hard of hearing, you stupid little fucker." He brought his face close to mine. "I've never liked you, and I don't owe you nothing."

He let go and turned away, walking back into the pub. So much for the new all-pals-together family. I waited till he'd gone in before heading that way myself to get Trish. As I reached the double doors and pushed the right-hand one, the left-hand one swung open and Trish came barrelling out. She looked angrier than the Dragon on a bad day.

"What's up?" I said. "You look like someone's killed your cat."

"Let's go George, come on, get moving." She was striding towards the Roller without looking back. I fell in behind, but couldn't keep up, what with the pains. By the time I got to the car, she was sitting behind the wheel staring straight ahead with jaws clamped tight.

I got in and she immediately drove fast out of the car park. It was a good mile or two before she calmed down and started driving sensibly. I waited for her to explain.

"I assume George," she said. "That your dear relative was not forthcoming with the cash?"

"That's right. Not too surprising I suppose, but what happened to you?"

"That fucking Alf only tried to rape me."

I thought perhaps she was exaggerating, but then thought it was possibly not the right thing to say under the circumstances.

"I went to the ladies when you went outside with Arthur and the bastard followed me in and tried it on."

"What did you do?"

"I picked up the ashtray by the basin and opened up the cut you prepared yesterday."

"That was handy," I laughed.

She smiled. "Now I think about it, it was quite funny. But what a fucker."

"Welcome to the Brittons."

"No thanks," she said. "You're welcome to them."

There was a pause as my mind turned to the current situation. I had the glimmering of an idea.

"You know this document we're trying to understand?" I said.

"Have you had a revelation?" she replied.

"Not about what it is, but we don't need to know," I said.

"How's that?"

"Sullivan and his friends obviously have something to

hide so we can get what we want without needing to understand it."

"So the big question is, what do we want?" She took her eyes off the road and smiled at me. "What do we want George?"

"I don't know about you but I want this fucking family out of my life," I said.

"Is that all?"

"No, I want a quiet life. I want all the aggro to stop. I want to relax without looking over my shoulder."

"All of that is just not wanting this," she said. "What about picturing what you do want?"

That pulled me up a bit. I realised that what I wanted more than anything was her. Her but not her as a wife. Her as I'd seen her that last few days. Fun, a mate, someone on my side. Of course, sex like the week before would be icing on the cake.

"Tell me something," I said.

"What's that then George?"

"What did that note mean?"

"What note?"

"The note with your phone number."

She glanced at me, paused, then laughed, "I just wanted you to know who it was from."

"But they knew at the desk who had left it."

"Lighten up George, it was just something to raise a smile."

I looked at her, her face was deadpan. Maybe she was right, but then maybe, maybe.

After a couple of minutes silence she said, "Back to the question of what we want from this situation, I think I can see a way of dealing with all your negativity."

"What's that then?"

"We need to head for Mill Hill, but first we need to protect ourselves."

"Against what?"

"Against the people named on that document who wouldn't want it getting out."

"So how do we do that?"

"We have to make sure that if anything happens to us, it goes to the papers, and we have to let them know that."

"We could put it in the Bullion," I said.

"Not sure if that's very safe what with Arthur casing the place. Tell you what, we could post it to ourselves just for now and then work out something better later."

"Well there's plenty of envelopes and stamps at the warehouse, let's head there."

As we drove, Trish outlined her idea of what we could do at Sullivan's house in Mill Hill. She really was a live wire, plenty between the ears. The best combination of brains, looks and spark I'd come across in a woman ever, I think. I sat there watching the road roll by, daydreaming about her and wondering if our crossed paths could stay crossed.

It felt good to have some idea of what we were doing. We drove towards the warehouse, only stopping at a petrol station for our hunger and the car's thirst. Two cold pasties is nobody's idea of a feast and we didn't even sit down to eat them. I didn't want the Roller to stink like Keith's van, so I insisted we eat out on the forecourt. To be fair, I think the smell of petrol probably improved the taste. After wiping our hands on the hard paper from the big roll, we got back in the car and moved on.

We entered the warehouse yard and stopped at the bottom of the office stairs. I went up and put the key in the outside door but couldn't turn it. I was fiddling about for a bit before I realised it was already open. That wasn't good. Maureen would never have left the place open. I opened the door slowly and stood stock still, listening. As I got used to the quiet, I started hearing the noises a building seems to make all by itself. I suppose it's the wind that makes for the creaks and rattles. Then, among those sounds I heard something else. It was coming from the actual warehouse downstairs.

I crept across the office to the top of the internal stairs and stopped to listen again. There was definitely a sort of ripping sound. I went down as quietly as I could and looked through the glass panel of the fire door. The rolls of carpet were on hangers set out in rows so I couldn't see the whole space. I quietly opened the door and heard someone muttering to themselves. I glimpsed some movement down one of the rows. Somebody seemed to be dancing, waving his arms around and swearing.

I got closer and saw that it was Davidson, with a Stanley knife in each hand, dancing down between the rolls of carpet slashing at them with the knives.

He was saying "Kill Dennis would you, you bastards? Well just see how you like this."

I looked around for a weapon but could only see an offcut of Berber lying on the floor. I grabbed it and rolled it up tight making a sort of pole about six foot long. I approached him.

"What the fuck do you think you're doing?" I yelled.

He stopped, turned around and ran at me with his eyes wide, flailing around like a windmill. I was glad I'd picked up the carpet. I stepped in towards him and, as soon as he was in range, shot the roll forward at his face. He fell to a sitting position on the floor, dropping the knives as he went down, his nose bleeding like a geyser. I pushed the knives away from him with the roll.

"You stupid cunt," I said, looking down at him. "What was that going to achieve?"

He just looked at me with a mixture of hatred and self-pity.

"The key," I said. "Give me the key. Right now." He moaned a bit but fished around in his pocket and handed it over.

"Right," I said. "Out, and don't bother coming back, ever. Oh, and don't expect to be staying at the Monarch at my expense any more."

He got to his feet, and holding his sleeve to his nose,

walked ahead of me up the stairs and out through the office.

I stood at the top of the stairs to make sure he left and as he headed towards the gate I shouted:

"And when the Brittons ask for their money off you, tell them Arthur's already taken it from me."

I went back into the office to grab an envelope and stamps, locked up and went back down to the car.

"Okay, let's get out of here," I said.

"What on earth was that about?" she said.

"Your sweet friend William Bloody Davidson was taking revenge on us by shredding my carpets with Stanley knives."

"So what happened?"

I related the Berber defence/offence episode.

"Wow," she said. "What a stupid pillock. Well done you, George." She leaned over and put a kiss on my cheek. "Where to now?" she asked.

"Just drive towards Mill Hill and keep your eyes open for a post box," I said.

After a couple of miles she pulled over.

"There's one," she said.

"What's your address?" I said.

She told me and I wrote it on the envelope. I got out and strolled to the post box, crammed the large envelope into the slot and legged it back to the car.

"Okay, we're safe," I said.

"Don't bet on it," she responded.

"What do you mean?" I asked.

"If you want to fuck with the big boys George, prepare to get fucked," she said, pulling away from the kerb and steering towards Mill Hill.

We got there in about half an hour and drove slowly past one way to check out the house. There was nothing untoward and no cars out front but the lights were on so we turned at the junction and cruised back.

Trish stopped at the gates and I got out and went to the entry intercom. I pressed the button.

"Who is it?" came the metallic voice.

"George Healey," I said.

There was a long pause.

"Wait a minute," came the voice.

I went back to the car. After at least a couple of minutes, the gates swung open and Trish eased the car forward through the gates towards the house. As we came to a standstill a figure emerged from the shadows holding a shotgun. It looked like the bodyguard from the previous night. He had a massive bruise on his forehead.

"This way," he said, waving the gun towards us.

We went towards the front door and the guard fell in behind us.

"Is Mr Sullivan at home?" I ventured. It's amazing how polite you get with a shotgun behind you.

"Shut up," came the voice. "Go inside."

We did as we were told but once in the hallway, waited till he said, "Go left."

It was like one of those spot-the-difference puzzles. Everything almost the same but paintings missing, Sullivan looking somewhat more relaxed, no Mrs Sullivan looking petrified, no Brittons.

Sullivan got up, looked at us and said: "What's your problem Healey? Why do you keep disturbing my peace?"

"I came by to check that you'd spoken to Special Branch about tomorrow's party," I said just to wind him up.

"You know damn well I have. You've got me over a barrel."

"I've come to offer you something you'll like," I said.

"What I'd like is you and your friends out of my life."

"Well that's the point really, they're not actually friends of mine and it strikes me that you're not looking forward to seeing them at your office party."

He looked at me with his head cocked, "Go on fella, this is beginning to sound like music to my ears."

"It strikes me also, that you quite like the pictures you rashly sold so cheap last night." He was looking really interested now. "So, if the people who have your pictures didn't have their documentation or receipts, and you did, it could very much look like they'd been stolen, wouldn't you say?"

"You're damned right it would," he said. "But why wouldn't they have the paperwork?"

"Because I have it all," I said, then continued, "I also have the three addresses where you'll find the pictures."

"Jeez Healey, they really aren't your pals are they? But what are you getting out of this?"

"I'm getting my money for the carpet, at the revised price, as a draft, first thing in the morning. I'll trade the receipts and the addresses for the draft."

"You think you can play hardball with me? What if I don't?" he said belligerently.

"You know perfectly well what will happen if you don't. Copies of your little secret go to the Stock Exchange and the City press. Oh, and by the way, that will be triggered automatically if anything happens to either, or both, of us." I glanced at Trish and she gave me a smile.

I carried on:

"Given how confident they were about their friends in Special Branch, I suggest you get on to a different lot about the paintings. You'll know where the pictures are, and you'll know where the thieves will be. What time is the grand visit?"

"It's scheduled for midday, everyone has to be in place by eleven."

"I suggest you rustle up that draft on the dot of nine then. It still doesn't leave you much time."

"You're not kidding," he said. "Can't we do it earlier?"

I thought about it. If he passed the info to the coppers too soon they might do an early raid which I could get caught up in. I couldn't really disappear first thing from the house given how the Dragon would no doubt be hyped up about the event and wanting endless confirmation of her regality.

"Eight o'clock, on the dot," I finally said. "Trish here will bring the paperwork and do the swap. The Brittons will get there about ten thirty."

"I'm looking forward to seeing them again," he said. "With the tables turned."

We drove back towards home discussing the timings of the morning. Trish dropped me off after reassuring me for the umpteenth time that she'd wake up well in time to get down to McCains by eight and straight back to the house to pick up me and the Dragon.

She drove off and I was pleased to see no sign of Steph's car as I headed for the front door.

"Ah, there you are George. I suppose you've been out drinking all afternoon," she started, then continued, "Did you meet up with Alf and Arthur?"

I made a non-committal noise.

"Have you sorted yourself out for the morning then?" I asked her.

"Oh yes," she beamed. "I'm going for peach. Steph thought lemon would be more appropriate but I wasn't having any of it. The peach it is, with my pearls."

I forced a smile. "Terrific, so we can just get going in the morning without any dramas?"

"Of course, why would there be? I sincerely hope you've organised the Rolls for us?"

I told her I had, and the evening carried on in that vein, with the Dragon wanting to know how she should address the Queen, whether to curtsy, whether to smile. On and on it went so I switched on the telly and let everything wash over me till I could plausibly go to bed.

I woke up early the next morning worrying about the day's arrangements. The Dragon was already busying herself in the bathroom. I went down to the kitchen in a robe to get some coffee. While I waited for the kettle to boil, there was a ring at the doorbell. I nearly shat myself thinking it was the coppers. I legged it to the study window where I could see out the front of the house without being seen. I looked out but there were no rozzers, just a bloke standing on his own wearing skin-tight trousers and a yellow shirt with puffy sleeves.

I went to the door and opened it.

'Yes?" I said.

He looked at me, "I am Raymonde. I've come to create Beryl's hair." He went to walk past me but I blocked his way.

"You piece of shit," I snarled. "You've caused me so much fucking grief, I've a good mind to pop you one."

"On the contrary, I think you are the piece of shit. You don't appreciate Beryl at all. She is a beautiful, creative and generous person. You are a small-minded little bourgeois," he said.

The Dragon came storming up behind me, "Get out of the way George, I can't possibly appear before Her Majesty with my hair not done right. Come on Raymonde, come in. Don't mind George, he's been a bit stroppy lately."

"Asshole," he hissed at me as he barged past.

203

"Oh, George," said the Dragon. "Get Raymonde a coffee if you please. Milk and three sugars."

I went back to the kitchen, drank my coffee and made a second one. On my way to the Dragon's room I detoured to the bathroom and put a large slug of laxative in it. When I went to put it down where he was primping and preening I made sure I spilled some on his hideous shirt.

I got myself dressed with the few remaining things I'd left at the house and went downstairs to wait. The hairdryer droned on upstairs.

Eventually it stopped and the Dragon came downstairs just as the Roller pulled up by the front door. I wanted to ask Trish how things had gone but when I opened the front door the Dragon swept by me heading for the car. Trish was only just able to get out and open the door before the Dragon reached it. She smiled sweetly and said, "Good morning, Mrs Healey."

The Dragon cut her dead.

As she opened the other door for me, I searched her face for some clue about McCains but she just smiled and said: "Good morning Mr Healey."

We drove for a few miles with me trying to catch Trish's eye in the rearview mirror, desperate to find out if all was going to plan when I heard sirens. I looked around, but they weren't behind us. They got louder and then came into sight heading towards us, headlights blazing. Trish looked unconcerned, as did the Dragon, but I was shitting myself yet again.

Three jam sandwiches came by at a hell of a rate, rocking the Roller as they did so and then calm returned. I thought they might have been for some accident or assault, but then there wouldn't have been three, so I suspected that Trish had handed over the receipts and addresses, but had she got the draft? I looked back at the mirror but Trish was giving nothing away. The Dragon just looked like she was wetting herself with excitement.

We hit the City and Trish headed for Cheapside but when we got there it was blocked by a barrier with City police turning everyone away. We stopped and one of them came over to us. He went to the driver's window which Trish lowered.

"Can't come by here until later today," he said, leaning close into the window. "You'll have to find another way around."

"But, these are guests.." Trish started, when the Dragon leaned over the back of Trish's seat and interrupted:

"We have an appointment to meet the Queen, we have to get through."

He looked at her steadily. "I don't care if you are the Queen, my instructions are to let no vehicles through. I suggest you get out and walk Madam."

The Dragon threw herself back into her seat like a petulant child.

"Right," she said through gritted teeth. "Come on George, get out, we're walking."

Trish leapt out to open the door for her. I just had time to tell Trish to park the car somewhere and then come to the building on foot and wait outside.

I took a last glance at Trish. "Certainly Mr Healey, have a nice time," she smiled.

The Dragon marched off down the road hissing "Keep up

George, we can't be late."

It only took a few minutes to walk to number seventy-eight but the Dragon was bitching about the inconvenience and lack of respect the whole way.

When we got to the building there was a handful of City coppers outside. The Dragon went to barge through but a sergeant blocked her way.

"No visitors today I'm afraid Madam."

She puffed herself up, "I am a guest at this event."

He turned to another uniform, "You got the guest list there constable?" he said.

The constable came closer, "Name?" he asked.

"Mr and Mrs George Healey," she said like she was the Queen her fucking self.

He looked down the list "Healey, Healey, Healey," he muttered, his finger going down the names.

"We're special guests," she chipped in.

He folded over the page, "Ah, the special guests, yes," he said. "There you are." He looked to the Sergeant. "They're on the special guest list Sergeant."

The sergeant turned to another constable. "Constable Peters, escort these good people to the special reception area."

We followed the plod into the building. As we walked across the reception area I couldn't help looking at the floor. The fitters had done a fantastic job. It looked majestic, bloody magic. I saw Freeman lurking near the desk and caught his eye. He looked away quickly. The PC led us past the desk and along a corridor, showing us into a boardroom with tea and coffee in the corner and a bowl of fruit on a big glass table.

The Dragon looked round approvingly. I went to take an apple. "Don't you dare touch that George," she warned me. A few minutes later, the door opened and in came Alf and Arthur, all suited and booted with their hair slicked down. Alf's certainly looked odd then I realised he'd combed it down his forehead to cover the damage I'd caused. They looked like a pair of kids just about to go on a birthday treat.

The door opened again and a pair of coppers came in. The first one piped up: "Hello lads, Beryl, how's it going?"

Alf and Arthur grinned and shook his hand. "Good to see a friendly face," said Alf. "How's it going yourself, Harry?"

"Nightmare, all this royal security bollocks," Harry replied. "Everyone these days is so bloody touchy, we have to play it by the book."

"Meaning what?" said Alf, looking suspicious. "We are going to be seeing Her Majesty aren't we?"

"'Course you are," Harry said. "We just have to do an individual interview and pat down for each of you. So who's up first?"

Arthur volunteered and went out of the room with them. We waited a few minutes and coppers returned, taking Alf with them this time.

"Where's Arthur?" said the Dragon as they left the room.

Harry turned and said over his shoulder: "Gone through to the reception line, you'll be joining him in a minute."

The Dragon started pacing up and down the room. "I don't like this George," she said. "It's not right, treating us like this, like common criminals."

"I'm sure it's fine," I said. "They just have to follow special rules when it comes to protecting the Queen. You wouldn't want any harm to come to her, would you?"

"I suppose you're right," she said doubtfully. Then she perked up, "It will be wonderful to see Her Majesty up close won't it? They'll be so jealous at home."

Just then the door opened again and Harry poked his head in and looked from the Dragon to me. "I'd do you together but rules is rules. Who's it to be?" he said.

I went to go with him but the Dragon barged in front of me and headed for the door.

"Now you behave yourself when we're out there George," she said as she left, "No picking your nose and you only say 'yes ma'am or 'no ma'am'. Got it?"

She left the room and suddenly a weight was lifted from me. I almost danced round the boardroom. I took an apple and bit into it. It was lovely. Sweet and juicy. I was savouring it when I heard a scream from another room. There were sounds of a scuffle and shouting and I could make out the Dragon's voice in among the noise. I took another bite and settled down in a comfortable chair.

There was a pause and then Harry came back into the room with the other copper. "Well George," he said. "I presume you've gathered what's going on?"

I nodded, swallowing a large chunk of apple.

"I should be charging you with aggravated burglary, assault and false imprisonment along with the others but it seems you have friends in high places."

I nodded again, to show willing, but I have to say I was just waiting for him to tell me to fuck off out of there. I was already thinking of the drive out of town with Trish in the Rolls.

"However," he said. 'However'? What the fuck did he mean 'however'? I looked at him like he'd just crapped on the floor.

"However," he repeated, "I don't think we can allow you to join the reception line. After all, you are just the carpet supplier, not a vital cog in the financial engine that is McCain Sullivan."

"You know what, detective inspector," I said. "I get it that I am about as welcome as a blister on a dick but how about letting me watch from a distance? I'd love to see Her face when She walks on that carpet."

"I suppose we could allow that, from a distance" he said. Then continued, "By the way, when we searched your house this morning there was a gentleman there, Raymond Blackstock. He swore he knew nothing about the paintings, claimed to be a hairdresser. We pulled him in anyway, do you have any information about him?"

"He's an art dealer," I said. "Crooked as they come. He was there to appraise the painting. My missus wanted to sell it as fast as possible. To be honest, I didn't trust him myself. I don't think he's too fussy about provenance."

So there I was, positioned at a vantage point above the reception area a while later. I could just see the street from where I was. I looked down on the reception line and noticed that Sullivan and Pevsner were there at the end of the line nearest the street. There was a flurry of activity at the front of the building.

A limo drew up and was immediately surrounded by police and officials. From my vantage point I could see a small figure in pale blue with a matching hat coming into the building. How anyone at ground level could see, I've no idea. The figures around her parted as she walked across to the reception line. I don't know what I was expecting but it was just a well-dressed, middle-aged lady smiling and shaking hands with Sullivan and his crew. What a lot of fuss about nothing, I thought.

I turned away and found my way out of the building at the back. I walked around to the front where a crowd of gawpers were being kept behind barriers by the coppers. I caught sight of Trish and made my way towards her. As I approached, she turned and her face broke into a smile. I took her arm and guided her out of the throng.

"Hello George, fancy seeing you here," she said. "You wouldn't believe what you've been missing!"

"Did you get the draft?" I asked.

"There's been all sorts of comings and goings, I could have sworn I saw your family being herded into a police van!"

"I bloody hope so. Did you get the draft?"

"Do you really think I would hang around here if I hadn't?" she said. "I'm not exactly a royalist."

"Where's the Roller? Where's the draft?" I was beginning to get desperate.

"Oh, they're both safe. The car's just a couple of minutes up here." she said, pointing where we were walking anyway.

"And the draft?"

She smiled, "Oh, it's safe."

"Yeah, but safe where?"

"Oh George, I think perhaps you care more for the money than you do for me."

Put in that light, I was suddenly torn. She stopped and turned to face me, pulling the corner of a folded piece of paper out of her inside jacket pocket.

"George, you know what? You worry too much," she said,. "Now let's get away from this horrible place and its horrible people."

The car was where she'd said. We got in and got going. Once the traffic had eased up I said: "What in particular have you got against the City boys?"

She didn't answer immediately but looked into the distance as if calculating something. Eventually, she said "It's complicated, but someone I cared for a lot topped himself because of something they did."

"That's a bugger," was all I could think of to say.

"Anyway, I don't want to talk about it right now. Where

shall we head for?"

"Back to the hotel I suppose." I'd been so geared up to the result of the Queen's carpet thing that I hadn't really thought about anything after it.

"No, tell you what, let's pick up the Jag. They said it was ready a couple of days ago."

"That was quick," she said. "Feeling nostalgic are we?"

"I've been feeling nostalgic about that evening ever since it happened."

"Well it's good that it's mended already. Anyone would think you had Dave doing it."

"Yeah, can't have done much actual damage going into that ditch."

"So where is it?" she asked.

"Over near Harpenden, Shenks Bodies."

"Setting the course for Harpenden, Captain."

"I suppose after we've got the Jag, I should go and pay the draft into the bank."

I thought about how the draft would make everything fall into place. I could pay the fitters, pay off the gold card, pay off the overdraft and set about leaving the Dragon. Whether it was with Trish or without, at least I now knew what I wanted rather then just being told what to do, what to have, what not to have.

We arrived at Shenks and found the Jag looking pristine but I looked from the Jag to the Roller and knew where my heart lay.

"Can you drive the Jag back to the Monarch?" I asked her.

"Not so nostalgic then George?" She smiled.

"Tell you what, let's get a tea before we split up," I suggested.

"There's always a good caff near a garage," she said. "I'll ask them."

So we walked down the road a hundred yards to the Chequers Cafe - 'Tea's Coffee's All-Day Breakfast served all day'. We found an empty, formica-topped table and ordered a pot. As we waited, I looked at the patterns of wiped grease on the table.

"So these City boys that caused you this grief, they're on that document of Sullivan's aren't they?"

She looked daggers at me, then softened, "Yes. They took him for everything he had. They didn't need to, they just did it because they could. When he complained, they just said he was 'collateral damage'. Bastards."

"So if that document got to the papers, they'd get their comeuppance?"

"I think they would."

I considered the options, then said: "I think we should post it."

"That's big of you," she said, then thought for a moment. "The thing is, they're only two of the names on those documents. Sullivan and the others have nothing to do with it."

"Perhaps they're just going to be collateral damage." I said.

"For that," she said. "I'll drive the Jag."

The tea came in a metal pot that spilled all over the table top and the saucers. It was horrible too. Scalding hot and completely tasteless. We might as well have had hot brown water.

Trish went quiet for a while, obviously thinking hard.

"You do realise," she said, frowning. "That if we do post it, they'll be out to get you?"

"You don't think my brothers-in-law and wife won't be out to get me?" I said. "With the sort of briefs they have, they'll be out on the street in no time. I don't think there's going to be much of a life for me around here."

"It may not seem like it, but those City boys are a lot nastier, and vindictive too," she said.

"Well then, in for a penny, in for a pound. Perhaps it would be a good idea to keep the draft away from the bank for the moment," I said, "I hope those things work abroad."

We went back and signed the paperwork for the Jag then drove in convoy back to the Monarch. As we went through reception, the girl (Sarah? Claire?) said: "Good afternoon Mr Healey. Good afternoon Miss Trish".

We headed for the room and I lay on the bed feeling completely washed out. I felt done in mentally but strangely better around the ribs and pretty much normal down below. Trish sat on the side of the bed.

"Hey you," she said. "Any room for me to lie down too?"

I moved off the centre of the bed and she swung her legs up and lay beside me. We stared at the ceiling.

"George," she started. "How are you feeling?"

"Totally done in," I said.

"So you're not interested in a little cuddle?"

"I'm not sure I'm safe for a little cuddle," I said.

"Oh, I'm sure a little cuddle won't hurt anyone," she said, and snuggled up against me.

Now I have to say, I suddenly felt a bit less done in. A twitch here and there and a spark of interest. She moved up on one elbow, then leaned over and kissed me on the lips. I kissed her back and a wave of healing warmth ran through my body. She ran her hands down my body, I held her breast through her jacket.

She eased off my trousers and jacket before quickly taking off her own.

Now I have to say that over the years I've become quite an expert in the self abuse department. I know what I like and I know what feels good but honestly I had no idea. She did things that I had never even thought of. Not only that but she knew exactly when to stop, to let me calm down a bit before driving me crazy again.

I was moaning with anticipation but she climbed on top of me with her knickers and shirt still on and gyrated gently on me. I pulled her down towards me to kiss her again and feel her gorgeous tits through her blouse. She pulled away to sit and then turn and continue her manual torture. I was powerless. Wave after wave of pleasure ran through me. I relaxed totally and felt better than a pools winner.

There was a stillness as we lay there. I started to breathe deeply. I drifted off.

It must have been a while later that Trish gently woke me.

"Come on sleeping beauty, if we're going to send off the document, we'd better get it posted before we bottle out."

"Huh?" I said, "Oh. Yes. The second copy's at the warehouse. Give me a minute to wake up. What time is it?"

"It's just gone five-thirty. Don't worry, I can go down there and get it. You could probably do with a rest."

"It'll be shut up now unless Keith just happens to get back off a job."

"Have you got the key?"

I gave her the key and explained Maureen's security system.

As she was leaving the room, I stopped her, "Trish," she turned. "Can I have the draft?"

"You've already got it George, I put it in your pocket earlier." She blew me a kiss.

I lay back on the bed thinking I'd died and gone to Heaven.

I must have drifted off again because the phone by the bed woke me with a start. I was alone. I glanced at my watch, six-forty-five. I picked it up.

"Hello?"

"Hello George." Oh fuck, I thought. It was the Dragon.

"Hello Beryl, where are you?" I said, hoping she'd say locked up.

"Oh, I'm at the warehouse," she said. "Tidying up some bits and pieces."

"What do you mean?" The Dragon was a royal pain, but she generally steered clear of the warehouse. It sounded iffy.

"This and that," she replied. "Oh, and if you want to see your whore again, you'd better come down and say goodbye to her now."

"What the fuck are you talking about Beryl?"

"Do you really think I'm that stupid?" she said. "I know what you've been up to, and I don't appreciate you dropping me in it either. Just get down here now."

She rang off.

I got myself dressed in a hurry and legged it down to the Roller. As I drove, I tried to imagine what piece of nastiness the Dragon might have come up with. If she was out, did that mean her fucking brothers were too? It didn't bear thinking about. Cross Beryl and you got grief, cross the brothers and the grief turned nasty, I really didn't need to remind myself.

I was hoping against hope that they hadn't wriggled out on bail. What was this about Trish?

I pulled into the yard. There was just my Jag and her BMW parked there by the bottom of the office stairs so I put the Roller on the other side. I went up the stairs to the office door. It was open. I went cautiously through the office. It was deserted, I didn't know what the Dragon was up to but I suspected she meant to do me harm. I looked around for something to defend myself. There was a small fire extinguisher by the door to Maureen's office so I picked it up, hefted it in my hands and thought it would do as long as she hadn't got her hands on her brothers' guns. I crept down the internal stairs.

I couldn't see any sign of anything wrong through the fire door so I went in. It smelled of petrol. As I walked across the floor my angle of view changed and I saw Trish in the central cross-aisle, tied to an office chair. I went to get her but the Dragon's voice came from an aisle to my left.

"Stop right there George," she said. "You fucking snitch. I don't know what you were thinking but you crossed a line today."

I looked away from Trish and saw the Dragon, pouring petrol onto the rolls of carpet.

"Beryl," I shouted. "What the fuck are you doing?"

"Thought you'd get rid of me did you George? You should have thought it through. I was out on police bail after a couple of hours. Unfortunately, the boys have a bit more previous than me so it's going to take them a day or two."

She'd gone potty. She was right about me not thinking it

through though. I moved a little towards Trish. I could see that she had a hankie stuffed in her mouth.

"I wouldn't go any closer to Patricia if I were you, there's a pool of this petrol under that chair and I've got a lighter in my hand."

I could see the pool under the chair, leading to other pools around the floor.

"What are you hoping to get out of this Beryl? It can't end well for anyone."

"As long as it ends badly for you, I'm not fussed," she said. "You bastard. You even had to drop Raymonde in it didn't you?"

Just then, there was a movement behind me. I glanced back to see Keith sauntering up behind me casually smoking a fag.

"Hello all," he said. "What's going on here?"

"For Christ's sake put that fag out Keith, the place is full of petrol!"

"I wondered what that smell was," he said.

I whipped the cig out of his mouth and flicked it in a high arc over the top of Trish, straight at the Dragon. It was a good shot, the petrol around Beryl went up with an enormous whoomph. She screamed and dropped the can, splashing herself, the flames jumped onto her. The carpet rolls all ignited. The screaming got louder.

Suddenly, the flames were taking hold all around. Snakes of fire leaping gaps and jumping all over the floor. Everything turned into slow motion as I saw with horror the fire getting closer to the office chair. I launched myself at Trish setting off the extinguisher as the pool around her feet ignited. The powder damped the rising flames but I was moving too fast to stop. I hit her full on and we careened down the cross-aisle on the office chair and crashed through the fire exit onto the loading bay and off the edge into the yard. Keith came tumbling out after us followed by a colossal wall of flame which licked around the cars there, stripping the paint off. The screams had stopped.

I pulled the cloth out of Trish's mouth while Keith produced a Stanley knife out of his tool belt and cut the cords.

"Are you okay?" I asked her. She coughed and spluttered, nodding.

"I reckon I owe you one," she said.

"We need to get away from here and find a phone," I said as I helped her across the yard away from the building.

"I wouldn't worry about a phone," said Keith. "Give it a couple of minutes and the fire service will see the flames from their station."

I glanced up and the office was already belching smoke from windows that were shattering with the heat.

"I'd move the van if I were you Keith," I said. "You need to look after the only asset of Healey Carpets now that you're running it."

He laughed, but all the same moved the van further away. I helped Trish to the Roller and reversed straight out of the yard bouncing onto the road.

We drove a couple of hundred yards from the building then stopped and looked back. Keith had been right, the whole place was an inferno. I looked at Trish, she practically jumped on me, covering me with kisses and then bear-hugging me. I winced slightly but the pain was worth it.

She sat back in her seat and stared silently at the flames then tears started pouring down her face. She started sobbing then taking deep gulps of air. She beat a drumroll with her fists on the dashboard then calmed down a bit and sat still, taking short breaths. Finally, she leaned over and kissed my cheek.

"Did you get the document from the filing cabinet?" I asked her.

She shook her head.

I glanced back at the office as it collapsed.

"Oh well, one day can't make too much difference. We'd better head for your place to get the other one when it arrives in the post tomorrow. We can always fax it to the papers."

"What then?" she said.

"Well I need to pick up my passport from the Monarch, but I think we should go somewhere for a dance."

"A dance?" she laughed. "Hasn't dancing got you in enough trouble?"

"That's a chance I'm happy to take," I said. "Do you fancy learning to tango in Buenos Aires?"

"Oh good God George," she said laughing. "What a bloody wonderful idea, but what about your business?"

"What business?" I said as we pulled away and the flames faded in the rear-view mirror.

END

39813839R00126

Made in the USA
Charleston, SC
18 March 2015